Here Today, Scone Tomorrow

Baker's Rise Mysteries Book One

R. A. Hutchins

Cover Design by Molly Burton at cozycoverdesigns.com

ISBN: 9798470117557

For everyone who, like me,
loves to curl up and get cosy with a great book!

CONTENTS

If you follow this list in order, you will have made a perfect batch of fruit scones to enjoy while you read!

ONE

Stan Houghton stormed out of the front door of the manor house known as 'The Rise' and strode off down the gravel driveway. His face, a molten red from his latest showdown with the 'lord of the manor' Harold Baker, contorted into a furious visage which matched his balled fists and heavy breathing. Surprised to see a familiar figure, dressed to the nines, approaching from the other direction, Stan tried to rein in his temper whilst making pleasantries.

"Good morning, Mrs. Edwards, fine day," he did not pause even for a second as they passed each other, nor did Stan listen for a reply as he hurried off back to the farm.

"If that's you again Houghton, you can get lost!" the shouted warning from indoors could be heard behind the flaking wooden main door of the manor, as its next visitor waited patiently on the doorstep.

"Oh, hello," his greeting was hardly welcoming even when Harold did pull the door open, "you'd better come in then!" He stalked into the main drawing room, eyeing his pet parrot suspiciously as if an outburst might ensue, and muttering, "not a word," as Harold waggled his finger in the direction of his feathered friend's perch.

The parrot, taking only one fleeting look at the outstretched finger, and choosing to also completely ignore the hastily given warning, screeched, "Old trout! Old trout!" and rose from his perch, flapping his wings viciously around the head of the woman who had just entered the room.

"Enough!" Harold said sternly, and the parrot finally decided to cease his assault.

"I gather this isn't a great time? I suppose Farmer Houghton was commenting on your latest rent increases for the village?" The woman tried surreptitiously to restore the elaborate up-do which the stupid parrot had managed to make look like a bird's nest. Giving up, she continued, "With the number of fields he has, I'd wager he's sorely affected." She stated it as a matter of fact, apparently unmoved by either the rent situation or the plight of a neighbour.

"Aye, well, he's always here threatening when the prices go up, but he pays it in the end. Just like they all do, if they want to keep living in Baker's Rise."

"Quite so. Anyhow, I've been baking and thought you might like a scone or two?"

Harold tried to hide his surprise. It was not a common occurrence for villagers to make their way up the hill for anything other than to air their gripes, let alone such a comely example of womanhood. For a moment, Harold was lost in sweet reminiscence of his many dalliances in years gone by. He was old now, stout in the waist and grizzly of feature, so he very much doubted that was what was on offer here. Nevertheless, he was intrigued as to what exactly would warrant such a special visit.

"Thank you kindly, dear lady, please take a seat and I will prepare a pot of tea," Harold licked his lips as he took in the sight of her, her face all made up to show her features at their best, her body encased in a tight tweed suit. When the lady didn't immediately sit, he was confused for a moment, until he realised that she would need to perch on top of one of the many mounds of paperwork, old magazines and newspapers which littered every available surface. Quickly, Harold swept a pile of brochures from the end of a settee and rushed off to the kitchen.

When he returned, the scones were arranged on one of the fine china plates, inherited from his mother, and which were stored in glass-fronted cabinets all around the room. Jam and butter – which she must have brought with her – sat in two dainty dishes complete with a miniature silver spoon and knife. *Aye, she's after something*, Harold thought to himself, his mind whirring with what he might get in return, as he set the tray on the small walnut coffee table between them, also cleared of its mound of papers hastily, and took his usual seat on a sagging Chesterfield.

"Shall I be mother?" she said coyly, fluttering her eyelashes at him.

Harold almost blushed like a schoolboy, "Indeed, madam, thank you kindly."

As she poured the tea and added the five sugar cubes which he requested, Harold thought he detected a small tremor in the lady's hands. Assuming it was a nervous anticipation for what was surely about to pass between them, Harold bestowed upon her his most gracious smile, which some rather ungrateful females

4

had in the past told him more resembled a leer. Accepting the cup and saucer gratefully, and the proffered scone, Harold settled back into his chair.

"So, my dear, what brings you up here?"

Instead of answering, the woman simply looked on as Harold's hand reached to his mouth and he took a huge bite of the baked treat.

"You do," she whispered, as Harold felt his breath begin to shorten, his chest to tighten, his tongue to swell and his throat to close.

The dropped plate smashed on the parquet floor, as Harold grasped his throat and managed to gargle, "What the..?" He staggered towards his guest, who simply moved out of his range.

"Peanut," she spoke clearly and with a sadistic smile, as Harold noticed for the first time the smudge of bright red lipstick on the woman's teeth, as if it had been applied by someone unused to doing so. It made her look like one of those clowns in a horror film. Why he would notice that, of all things, in this moment, Harold wondered as he collapsed to the floor, his body convulsing.

The last things he saw were her stilettoed feet stepping

over him as the woman went to retrieve the rest of the scones, and the china cups and saucers for washing. She reached down to check Harold's pulse, giving a nod of approval as she found none, before quickly collecting up the fallen remnants along with the broken pieces of crockery, and leaving the room silently.

Naught could be heard but the ticking of the antique grandfather clock in the corner and the squawk of the parrot, shouting "Peanut" on repeat.

TWO

Ten Months Later

Flora looked around her at the six small tables, all set out with fine china cups and saucers in co-ordinating colours, lace doilies, floral tablecloths and silver cutlery. She smiled to herself, content in all she had achieved since coming to Baker's Rise a few months ago. The tearoom in the old stables, closed up for several years, had been given a new lease of life with a fresh lick of paint and bunting hung around the rough walls. A new sign had been hung outside the door, advertising the 'Tearoom on The Rise' – Flora liked to keep things simple and elegant. She ran her hands down her neat apron and patted her hair to ensure she was as smart as possible, before checking her watch for the fifth time in as many minutes. Still half an hour remained till opening time. The local baker, George

Jones, had dropped off the day's delicacies an hour ago, and Flora had already arranged them in the display cabinet and fridge. Scones with clotted cream from the local farm and jam from the farm shop, teacakes, iced buns, custard tarts... a whole list of tempting treats for what Flora hoped would be her many customers, keen to try out the new tearoom on opening day. Flora wished to be baking some of the goods herself before too long, once she'd found someone in the village to teach her. She would start out as easily as possible, she had decided, and try to perfect the traditional English scone.

Flora had advertised the tearoom's opening in the local parish newsletter, the aptly titled, "What's on the Rise in Baker's Rise," as well as on the church notice board. She had tried to spread the news by word of mouth too, though this was more difficult as Flora was new to the village. She had quickly realised that folk here were not too keen on newcomers. Trust had to be earned, and civility only turned to friendship when you had embedded yourself suitably in village life. Flora hoped desperately that this would be a quicker process for her than for most, since she wished the tearoom to become a hub of village life. Mindful that any customers would have to travel halfway up the small hill, The Rise, to reach her, she had already thought about special offers

and loyalty schemes to tempt people her way.
Probably getting ahead of herself, Flora knew, but after
coming from a fast-paced and highly structured job as
an actuarial consultant in the city, she was already
struggling to fill her days and occupy her quick mind.

The bell on the door chimed and Flora was shocked
from her musings. It was still too early for customers.

"Flora? Are you here?" The polished tone of the local
solicitor, Harry Bentley, put Flora at her ease as she
rushed from behind the counter to greet him. His grey
hair popped around the door which he had only
opened a fraction, followed by his wide-rimmed
spectacles and his red, bulbous nose.

"Harry! What a lovely surprise!" the elderly gent, who
should have been long since retired by now but still
took an interest in the affairs of the village residents,
had been Flora's sole friend and confidant since she'd
arrived. It was he who had originally contacted her
about the estate, he who had advised she should keep
her true identity a secret until she had been accepted
by the villagers. Harry had arranged the refurbishment
of the coach house for Flora per her instructions from
London, and had suggested the tearoom as a viable
business opportunity. He had met her when she
arrived and had visited her several times since, always

with a friendly smile and a word of advice.

"Just thought I'd come to wish you luck on your first day, dear! Well, doesn't it look splendid! Very pretty indeed."

"Oh thank you, Harry, it wouldn't be anything without your recommendations and advice. Thank you for suggesting the farm shop, by the way, the jam and honey is delicious!"

"Not at all, my dear, now where are we with all the paperwork up at the big house?"

"Well, as you know there is mounds of it, I have only been able to shift the tip of the iceberg really. I know, it's my own fault. Being an actuary for so many years, I can't throw a single sheet of paper away without first reading what's on it! It makes the process slow and laborious, but I'm not in a hurry. The whole place is becoming dilapidated anyway. As you know, I've used the funds I could get my hands on to do up the coach house and this stable block. I'll have to wait to receive my divorce settlement before I can begin anything else. Hopefully, the villagers will have accepted me by then and it won't need to be so cloak and dagger," she gave a rueful smile and offered Harry a coffee from the new machine, which Flora had only just begun to learn how to use.

Eyeing the large silver monstrosity with distrust, Harry opted for a cup of tea, and sat down at the table nearest the counter.

"Aye, you've accomplished a lot in a few months, slow and steady wins the race especially in a place like Baker's Rise!"

"Indeed," Flora joined him at the table, a pot of tea for two and two toasted teacakes set in front of them. They chatted happily, until Flora looked at her watch and realised she should have changed the small sign on the door to 'open' some fifteen minutes ago. Not that she need worry, it was hardly as if she had a queue of customers waiting outside.

"I'll go and leave you to it. Remember to phone me if you need anything. On my home phone, mind, I still haven't worked out this mobile thing that my nephew gave me."

"Thank you, Harry," Flora busied herself clearing the table as she heard Harry's old BMW driving away on the gravel driveway. She took a deep breath, closed her eyes, and prayed that luck would be on her side and bring her some customers on her first day.

THREE

It was one thirty in the afternoon, and Flora was on the verge of giving up and closing for the day. She had hoped that by opening on a Saturday, she would attract some trade from those who were not working that day. Apparently she had been wrong. Sighing, she turned the coffee machine off at the wall, and walked to the other end of the small kitchen area to turn off the lights for this half of the room. Her mind on what she considered to be her abject failure, Flora was surprised to hear the small bell chime to indicate someone had entered the tearoom.

"Good afternoon," she quickly plastered a smile on her face, to replace the look of defeat she had worn all morning, and was met with the charming features of a man about her own age.

"Good afternoon, I thought I would try out our lovely

new tearoom that everyone's talking about!"

"Really? I mean, that's great, please take a seat. Are they really talking about it in the village?" Flora couldn't help herself, her curiosity got the better of her as per usual.

"Well, I mean to say," he blushed a deep shade of red and Flora realised the poor man had just been making pleasantries. Apparently she was great at scaring off customers, not so good at attracting them, "well, no, I saw your advert in the parish newsletter actually."

He looked so embarrassed, Flora felt awful, "Well, I'm Flora, Flora Miller, and I'm very pleased to meet you," she held out her hand and saw the man's look of relief as he shook it gently.

"Philip – Phil – Drayford, very pleased to meet you. I'm a teacher at the small village primary school."

"Lovely to meet you, Phil, what can I get you?" Flora fumbled in her large apron pocket for the unused notebook and pen she had stashed there for this very purpose, and tried to look professional. In truth, her hands were shaking and she could feel droplets of sweat forming on her brow. Feeling self-conscious, she raked her spare hand through her brown bob, aware that it was growing out now. When she'd lived in

London, Flora had kept her eight-weekly appointment at the hairdressers religiously. Now it had been several months, and both the longer length and the greys were beating her.

Taking a deep breath, Flora felt the pressure she was putting herself under. She really needed to pull herself together if she was going to make a success of this.

Her first attempt at a latte was a mess which Flora quickly threw down the sink. She had practised with this machine, but apparently when put on the spot she couldn't quite remember the many steps of the coffee-making process. Despite spending years under extreme pressure advising banks and investment houses.

Come on, Flora, it's a cup of coffee for goodness sake! she chided herself. She really should have just opted for a traditional cafetiere and served filter coffee instead. Eventually a sweating and irritable Flora managed to present a drink to Phil which somewhat resembled the coffee he had asked for, to go with the custard tart which she noticed he had already eaten.

"Let me get you another," Flora offered, indicating his empty plate, "they need eating anyway."

"Oh, thank you, that would be lovely," he was very softly spoken and smiled up at Flora in a way that made her stomach do a little lurch. Being only newly divorced, she certainly wasn't looking for anything even close to a relationship, so she hurried away to the counter, flustered and embarrassed.

"So, are you employed by the new owner of the estate?" Phil asked between mouthfuls, "Now, that is something the whole village is talking about!"

"I well, yes, I'm running the tearoom," Flora stuttered over the words.

"Excellent, and have you ever met them, the new owner I mean?"

"Ah, no, no tell me about your job," Flora quickly tried to change the subject, feeling her face flush from his line of questioning.

They chatted more easily then, as Philip told her about the little school which had only twenty-six pupils, and was under permanent threat of closure from the local council. Phil was the full-time teacher, but another lady also worked there part-time. Flora made a pot of tea for them both, and took the seat which Phil offered at his table – funnily enough he didn't request another latte. There were no more customers, so she was happy to get to know him and learn what she could about her new neighbours.

"Well, if you want to learn how to bake a scone, then there are several women in the village who all vie to be the best in that department!" Phil gave a small chuckle as he began expanding on the hobby which apparently held a lot of kudos in the local community. "There's the vicar's wife, Enid Wright – always wins first place in the village fayre Scone Competition, though I'm not sure she'd willingly share her secrets! Then there's Betty Lafferty, leader of the local branch of the Women's Institute until last year and a strong contender in the scone leagues. Her constant competitive streak, especially when it comes to the vicar's wife, is a source of, um, entertainment, to some of us who frequent the local pub. The doctor's wife, Edwina Edwards bakes, too, but sees herself as above the local rivalries. She's quite a cold, distant woman, so I'm not sure you'd have much luck asking there. Then there's the farmer's wife, Lily Houghton, who always has a smile and a friendly word, I'm sure she'd love to help you. Yes, she's your best bet for sure!" He smiled, as if having solved a very difficult riddle and Flora smiled back, relaxing at last.

"Thank you so much, Phil, you have been a wealth of information!" she stood up to clear the crockery and

Phil stood too, his hand brushing hers as he rushed to help her, "Oh, thank you!" Flora blushed and let him carry the teapot to the counter. Perhaps her first day had not been a write-off after all.

FOUR

"That is enough, Peanut!"

For a bird which only ever said its own name, the parrot was certainly a noisy housemate. Flora had never had a pet before. Never had time for them. Even when she was a child with no siblings, her parents could not be persuaded to buy as much as a goldfish to keep Flora company. Books though, she'd had books aplenty, and she credited that for her love of reading today. Flora made a mental note to see if the village had a library, before adding some more food to Peanut's tray.

Flora had asked the local vet, Will Monkhouse, over to check the bird when she had first arrived. Startled to find that the parrot came as part of the package, and unsure what to do with the feathered foghorn, Flora had enquired as to how one fed such an animal, and what looking after one entailed. Will had been a jolly chap, happy to share what he knew about the species, though also regaling Flora with many anecdotes about cows, which he impressed upon her were the most appealing animals on his caseload. Indeed, Flora had been subject to a full hour's worth of the many diseases and predicaments which our bovine friends can endure, and barely five minutes of practical parrot-related help. Nevertheless, she nodded and smiled, nodded and smiled until the visit came to an end, and then resolved to learn anything further about birds from the internet or in books.

It being Sunday, and having been warned off opening on the Sabbath day by Harry Bentley, who advised her that the villagers were very traditional in that respect, Flora decided to attend the church service in the village for the first time since her arrival in the area. She was hoping to get to know people better, to make some friends and hopefully to entice some of them up to her tearoom the following week.

The Church of Saint Nicholas and Saint Peter took pride of place on the village green. Reverend Francis Wright had met Flora at the large, wooden doorway, extended his hand graciously and formally welcomed her to the parish. Flora had returned his greeting and made to move into the main chapel, but was prevented from doing so when the clergyman refused to let go of her hand, which was ensconced, somewhat unwillingly, in his larger, sweaty one.

"Did you know, Mrs. Miller, that in former times the tearoom donated a full half of its profits to the church roof fund?" he licked his lips in an off-putting manner and Flora suppressed a shudder.

"No, I ah, I did not know that. The tearoom has been shut for several years now, has it not?"

"Indeed, but the church roof is sadly on its last legs, and we must all do what we can," he emphasised the 'all' with a tightening of his hand on hers before the man let Flora go and she rushed on into the church thankful for the cool anonymity which it afforded her.

Where to sit, now that was a good question. Flora smoothed down the knee-length skirt of her tailored lilac suit and scanned the pews. She had no desire to sit at the front, under the beady eyes of the man she'd just met, nor did she wish to take a seat which was usually reserved for someone else. Spying the familiar profile of Phil Drayford as she made her way up the central aisle, Flora gave a silent sigh of relief. The musty smell of old carpet, and incense mixed with centuries of sweat increased the further into the building she ventured. Phil welcomed her with a beaming smile and

Flora immediately felt more at ease, sitting down next to him on the hard wooden bench. No creature comforts such as cushions or even a spare bible were evident in this holy house, a signal no doubt of the austerity of the place and its dire lack of funds. Certainly, Flora surmised, this was the impression the Reverend Wright wished to achieve.

As the man in question took to the pulpit, and all assembled arose for the first prayer and hymn, Flora scanned the dozen or so people present. She spotted Harry Bentley two pews ahead and to her left, and smiled back when he sent a subtle wink her way. There were several women, all in extravagant hats, as if one were trying to outdo the other with their millinery, apart from one woman. Sitting in a pew near to the back, with a portly man whose face looked like it could do with a good wash and shave, the woman sent a timid smile when Flora caught her eye. Short and with only a straw bonnet to accessorise her simple dress, she immediately struck Flora as the kind of woman she would like to befriend. The others, with their perfect hats and snooty dismissal of Flora's smiles, were likely the master bakers whom Phil had mentioned yesterday. Flora knew she would have her work cut out for her attracting them up the hill to the tearoom. *Never mind,* she thought to herself, *one day at a time.*

As the service ended, and Flora walked out into the welcome fresh air of the summer's day, chatting quietly to Phil about a newly-discovered, shared love of books, Flora's heart sank when she saw the vicar waiting to speak with her on the freshly-manicured lawn outside the church. She was just about to ask Phil to save her by offering her a lift back up to The Rise, when the friendly face of the straw-hatted woman popped up beside them. The vicar, seeing Flora already in conversation, moved reluctantly out of her path, and Flora felt the relief flood through her. A man to be avoided wherever possible, she felt, or else her meagre profits – of which there would be none for a while to come, Flora thought sadly – would already be allocated before she had even earned them.

"Good morning," the other woman seemed breathless, and her two chins wobbled as she came to a stop beside them. Phil made his polite goodbyes, and Flora introduced herself.

"Pleased to meet you, Flora, I'm Lily Houghton. Wife to Farmer Houghton, though he's had to rush back in the tractor for a pig emergency. I thought I'd introduce myself and say how happy I am that you've re-opened the tearoom. Such a shame when it closed so suddenly."

"I'm so happy to meet you, Lily, I haven't met many people from the village yet, and I'm keen to get to know everyone," Flora spied the vicar out of the corner of her eye, his hands gesticulating wildly at the roof as he spoke in animated tones to Harry Bentley. *Well, maybe not everybody,* she thought to herself, before chatting easily to Lily about scones and how she was desperate to bake her own. Flora deliberately skirted the issue of the 'pig emergency,' deciding that there are some things best left unknown!

FIVE

Flora had declined Lily Houghton's kind offer of Sunday lunch up at the farm, on the outskirts of the village, but had made plans to go up there after closing the tearoom on Monday evening for her first baking lesson. Flora was both excited and nervous in equal measure, but yearned for the day when she could sell scones which she herself had produced.

For today, though, she had grand plans to sort out some of her clothes in the coach house which now made a cosy home for her, before heading further up the hill to the manor house to do a couple of hours' work on sorting the paperwork there. No matter how long Flora spent sifting and filing, she didn't seem to even make a dent in the piles of papers strewn in the study, let alone in other areas such as the sitting room and what should have been the dining room, but which appeared to be a general dumping ground.

Flora had been so glad to make her escape from London and the rat race, to move to the countryside for a slower pace of life and for a fresh start. Having spent the past two decades working her way up in the City, marrying an investment banker, and having all the trappings which such a union entailed, Flora was looking for a quieter life. Her ex-husband and his latest paramour now lived in her seven bedroom Kensington home, though Flora should shortly be receiving her half of the divorce settlement, which would mean she could start the renovations on the main manor house. She had grand plans to turn it into a county house hotel, but for the moment, Flora would be happy with fixing the leaking roof, putting in new electrics and central heating, and making the place generally less of a health hazard. *One day at a time*, was her new favourite motto. Impatient by nature, Flora had a hard time sticking to this, and daydreamed of serving her own afternoon teas in a charming sitting room, whilst the piano was played expertly in the background and her guests surveyed beautiful, manicured lawns.

Dragging herself back to the half-eaten cheese sandwich which constituted her lunch, Flora wrapped it in cling film to save for later and looked morosely upon the many boxes and garment carriers piled up all

around her. Fashion had always been her weakness.
Clothes, accessories, all of the latest deigns and labels,
often acquired on holidays in the Med. Indeed, at her
home in London, Flora had enjoyed a walk-in
wardrobe of gargantuan proportions. Here, she had
one antique armoire and a narrow chest of drawers.
Flora had already unpacked the clothes she considered
most suitable for her new lifestyle, and now had to go
through the rest, forcing herself to part with years'
worth of beloved pieces. Of course, she could store
them at the manor house, but Flora was trying to begin
a new, more frugal way of living, and to discard any
items that held painful memories. She would donate
them to the two charity shops in the village – one
which supported the local cat and dog shelter, and the
other for Marie Curie Cancer Care. Flora was happy to
do this, she just didn't relish the prospect of going
through all of the pieces one by one.

Peanut flew from his perch and landed on her
shoulder. At first very wary of his sudden flights and
loud squawking, Flora had opted to keep him in the
big cage which had come down from the manor house
with the bird. It took up at least a third of the tiny
sitting room, and she rather resented the cage's
presence at first, as much as that of the bird himself,
until she realised that actually it was nice to have a bit

of company in the evening – even if the conversation on his side consisted of only one word. Peanut would sit with his head cocked, as if he could actually understand, as Flora detailed her plans for first the tearoom in the old stable block and then the manor house itself. She laughed at her own fanciful thought that the bird might be quite intelligent. Vet Will had thought him to be about fifteen, so Flora knew that if he hadn't picked up more than one singular word by now – his name at that – the feathered creature wasn't likely to suddenly start conversing. Nevertheless, she spoke slowly at times, and repeated phrases often, in the hope that he might cotton on. In the three months since she had been living here, Flora had become accustomed to opening his cage in the morning and having him fly onto her shoulder at will. She enjoyed the soft feel of his feathers against her cheek, and secretly wondered why she'd never had a pet before now.

One dress carrier sorted, Flora had lost all will to continue. She kept thinking that she might need something for this type of event, or that piece had cost too much to give away and had only been worn once… in the end, she had added four dresses to the charity pile, two summer dresses to her crammed wardrobe, and had left the rest laying haphazardly over the small settee. Peanut had watched her intently, and Flora had the idea he was wondering just what kind of human he'd been landed with!

Perhaps, she thought, she would have more luck up at the manor house. She could be objective there, put on the business head that had served her well all her working life, and proceed methodically to organise everything as she would if she were going through the accounts and paperwork of a FTSE100 company. Yes, Flora thought, a walk up the driveway and an hour or two of being productive was just what she needed to clear her head enough to return to this mess. As she slipped on her floral sandals, completely impractical but a favourite from a holiday in Venice two years previously, Peanut came to perch on Flora's shoulder once again.

"No Peanut, I'm going out, you know the rules, I don't want you to get lost!"

"Peanut! Peanut! Peanut!" The bird's shrieks became louder and more urgent, and Flora had to cover her ears with her hands to block out the noise. In the end, presuming the bird might recognise the area around the coach house and manor anyway, and not knowing whether he had been allowed to fly freely in the past, Flora had no choice but to give in to Peanut's demands.

As it was, she walked the whole way with him happily sitting on her —not once did he even stretch his feathers as if to fly away. His emerald green plumage shone in the late afternoon sun, and Flora actually found herself grateful of the company.

SIX

Flora entered the manor house by the small side door which she always chose. It was the easiest key to remember on the large ring which she'd been given, and also it avoided being seen by anyone. Not that Flora had ever seen anyone on her regular trips up here, it was private land after all, but she preferred to keep her visits secret for now. The Rise had never been held in good esteem by the villagers, she had been told, and Harry Bentley had warned Flora off revealing too much, too soon. So, she snuck into the building like a thief, and tried to turn on as few lights as possible.

Normally, Flora went straight to the study to begin her sorting, but today being such a beautiful midsummer day she walked straight past that room, along the dim corridor and into the large, front drawing room. This was by far the largest of the two reception rooms and was central to Flora's future plans. The space had at one time probably been quite grand. Now, it held a mis-mash of uncoordinated furniture, a large space where Peanut's cage had once stood – complete with parrot droppings and discarded seed shells underneath, which no one had bothered to sweep up. The whole place smelt of damp and mould. Scanning the room, Flora could tell which of the battered armchairs the previous resident had regularly used, by the fact that it was one of only two seats not covered in paperwork, yellowing magazines and old, brown newspapers. The other free seat was at the end of an old chesterfield settee, and was surrounded by a stream of similar sheafs piled up randomly where they had landed on the floor, as if they had simply been swiped off the couch to make room for a visitor. Between the two, was a walnut coffee table with a wobbly leg. This, too, was free of any paperwork or reading material, and looked starkly empty in the midst of the carnage which was the rest of the room.

Upon entering the room, the parrot flew from Flora's shoulder, startling her with his sudden movement. Going straight to the armchair which had clearly been his owner's favourite seat, Flora assumed the bird wanted to find some comfort by sitting there. She was surprised, therefore, to see him ignore the cushions on the seat and instead sweep down to the floor. After a few seconds of pecking, the bird emerged just as quickly, flying up to sit on the clear coffee table. In his beak he had a large crumb, which he placed carefully between his feet.

"Peanut!" he screeched, "Peanut! Peanut! Peanut!"

Flora recalled Harry Bentley telling her the local doctor had ruled the death was due to choking, and she wondered for a brief moment if this was what the elderly owner of the manor had been eating at the time of his demise. This was the only reason she could think of why the bird should choose this one random bit of rubbish out of all the refuse, food packets, teacups and plates dotted around the room. The bird was fixated on the crumb, moving it around gently with his large talons and never once taking his eyes off Flora.

The persistent smell of fungi and rotting damp mingled with that of old paper, caused bile to rise suddenly in Flora's throat. She went to the large bay window, opening the top two sections as wide as possible, and breathing in the fresh air which came through. The view from here was stunning and caught her attention, pushing out all morbid thoughts. She tuned out the increasingly more aggravated calls from the parrot behind her and looked at the hills in the far distance, bright green under an azure sky. The fields of the Houghton farm, neatly demarcated by trees and traditional stone walls could be seen below them, and then the buildings which made up the village of Baker's Rise. The grass of the village Green stood out clearly, as well as the duck pond which sat in its centre, and the stone cottages which surrounded it. The main street, known locally as Front Street, led down from the Green towards the bottom of the village, and hosted a selection of shops, from a ladies' boutique and hairdressers to the village post office and general store. At the bottom corner could be seen the roof of the local pub, The Bun in the Oven. From there it was a short walk along a country lane until one reached the turnoff that led to the tearooms, and travelling further up the hill one eventually reached The Rise manor house itself. Gulping in the small amount of fresh air, Flora decided she had spent long enough in this room for today. It was the first time she had seen the sitting room in the daylight, and she was dismayed by the amount of work that would be required to bring it up to the necessary standard for a hotel. Not to mention the costs involved.

Her dreams had taken a knock, for sure, and Flora slunk out of the room without looking back. She called repeatedly for Peanut to follow her into the study until the bird reluctantly left his crumb on the coffee table to come and join her, his anger evident in the annoying flicking of his wings in her face, and his irritated shrieks in Flora's ear.

SEVEN

Monday morning dawned drizzly and wet. The good old British weather could never be relied upon to have two decent days in a row! On top of that, the climate here in Northumberland, in the North of England, was so different to that which Flora was used to in the South. London would be baking in July, and here the days could still be quite cool.

Flora was used to getting up early for her old job, so was dressed and at the tearoom by seven, even though she would not open until nine o'clock. George Jones, the local baker who owned 'Baker's Rise Pastries and Pies' on one of the cobbled lanes off Front Street, arrived promptly at half past seven with her order for the day. Scones, crumpets, a large chocolate cake and a few iced cupcakes for any children or even adults with a sweet tooth. Flora, who had just finished her second cup of tea for the day and was trying, unsuccessfully, to make a cappuccino on the new coffee machine, was glad of the interruption.

"It's a bleak day to be sure," George said as he handed her the basket of goods and waited silently while Flora emptied them into the display cabinet and onto the small china cake stands on the counter.

"Indeed, where has the sun gone?" Flora replied politely, handing him back the wicker tray and instinctively pulling her thin cotton cardigan further around her shoulders.

Instead of leaving immediately, George hovered, sweating profusely and awkwardly hopping from one foot to the other. He gave the clear impression that he had something else to say.

"Was there something I can help you with?" Flora asked, suddenly feeling uncertain.

"Aye, well, it's just.. I mean, you're probably as much in the dark as the rest of us, but we were having a discussion in the pub last night," he paused, his breathing heavy and laboured as if he had walked up the hill and not driven in his van.

"Yes?" Flora had no idea where he was going with this. Why would they be talking about her? Other than she was a newcomer, a woman alone. Then it hit her. The rents.

"You see, I know you're just employed here – you are just an employee of the new owner aren't you?"

Flora didn't answer so after a long, uncomfortable moment he continued, "So, we were wondering if you have any information like, on whether the new owner, the new landlord, will be raising the rents? They're crippling as it is, for small businesses like us, you see, and the old bast… the old bloke who lived here afore kept putting them up each year, without fail. That mansion must be like Buckingham Palace, the amount of income he stole… he got, I mean, from us honest locals."

It sounded like a speech, no doubt rehearsed in The Bun in the Oven with the other shop owners last night. Flora knew that the late Harold Baker had owned most of the village, the homes, the land, the buildings, but her time spent sorting through the deceased gentleman's documents had yet to shed any light on what he had done with all the money.

"Well, Mr. Jones…"

"George, please lass."

"Thank you, George, well, I have no knowledge to share at the moment. I can only assume that you should keep paying until you hear any different," Flora smiled in what she hoped was a reassuring manner and opened the door to let him out, signalling the end of their conversation. She didn't mean to be impolite, but she felt uncomfortable with the topic of discussion, and made a mental note to speak to Harry Bentley that evening. Perhaps he could speak to the villagers in that solicitor-like way that he had, that used a lot of lofty terminology but actually told you very little about anything.

With the baker on his way back to the village, Flora was just about to lock the door and make another pot of tea, when the familiar red hue of the postal van came around the corner. Flora suppressed a shudder. She really hadn't hit it off with the village postie, Joe Stanton. He persistently – and Flora suspected deliberately – got her name wrong, which caused Flora's hackles to rise on every meeting with the man. But, more than that, she had suspected several times now that her post had been opened and resealed before Flora received it. The man was cocky, much like the bankers and insurers Flora was used to dealing with in her previous life, and seemed to always insinuate that he knew something about her which was secret information.

"Good morning, Mr. Stanton," Flora used her most professional, distant tone.

"Morning, Florrie love."

"It's Flora," she ground the words out through a forced smile. The man simply smirked, making Flora want to wipe the look from his face.

"Quite a few for you today, love, but that's to be expected, isn't it?"

"Is it?" Flora did not want to know what he was referring to. There he went again, making insidious accusations.

"Yes, you know, with all you've got going on?"

"Well, thank you," Flora stood blocking the doorway to the tearoom. She certainly wasn't about to invite the loathsome man in for a cuppa.

"Aye well, just you think on," he let the strange comment hang in the air between them as the man got back in his van and drove off. Feeling shaken by the encounter, Flora decided against trying to practice with the new coffee machine again. She would write a special offer up on the blackboard instead, cup of tea and a cake for two pounds fifty. That is, if she even got any customers in to take advantage of it.

EIGHT

The day had taken a turn for the better, when a family visiting the area had happened upon the tearoom and chosen to have refreshments there. Flora had happily busied herself serving them slices of chocolate cake and cream scones, the only disappointment being that the three adults had asked for fancy coffees. Vanilla lattes of all things. Flora had managed a passable-looking round of drinks on the third attempt, after much muttering under her breath at the cursed machine. She had resolved then and there to get someone in from the company to teach her how to use the stupid lump of metal. Anyway, with a burnt thumb for her trouble, Flora had managed to serve the customers and they left with smiles on their faces, so it couldn't have been that bad, she hoped. That was, until Flora discovered that each cup of coffee had barely been drunk. It put a cloud over her enthusiasm, so she shut up shop at four o'clock and tried to focus on her lesson with Lily Houghton that evening.

After a light salad, which left her hankering for something sweet, Flora decided to walk through the village and up the hill on the other side to the farm. She could have travelled in her Audi, but she had felt very conspicuous the few times she had driven since arriving here, and it had spent most of the past few months in a garage up at the manor. She really should give it a drive out to the nearest town to stock up again on groceries. The little shop in the village, 'Baker's Rise Essential Supplies', was fine for basics, but didn't offer much in the way of choice, as well as charging almost double that of the nearest supermarket.

It had turned into a lovely evening. The clouds which had made the first half of the day overcast had now moved on, and it was warm enough for only a light cardigan over her blouse. Flora wished she had not worn the kitten-heeled, red shoes, and had instead chosen something more suitable to walking a mile and a half, but it was too late to go back and change now. To distract herself, she thought about the phone call she had shared with Harry Bentley before leaving the house. Ever the pragmatist, he had told her to focus on building up a presence for the tearoom in the village and on being accepted by the villagers. He had dismissed any mention of land rents and monies owed with a grunt, saying things were in place until the renewals arose in two months' time, and he would not elaborate on anything more than that. Flora had managed to squeeze out of him that the rents were, indeed, exorbitant, and so she assumed the villagers were quite right to be worried about another price hike. Harry wouldn't be drawn on what Harold Baker had done with all this money, vaguely referring to 'ventures' and 'interests' but would not be pinned down on details. Flora had thanked him and silently decided she herself would do some digging up at the manor house the next time she was there. All of those papers must hold some interesting information, surely, more than the bills from the milkman and a receipt for medical-grade mouthwash, which were the kind of things she had found so far. If there was money squirrelled away, Flora intended to find it.

Lily Houghton was a lovely woman, who welcomed Flora with a hug and a regret that she hadn't come half an hour earlier for dinner – it was always tripe on Mondays and plenty to go around. Seeing Flora's twinset and chinos, she had absentmindedly rubbed her hands over her stained apron and tried ineffectually to fix her hair back into its pins, but she smiled and greeted Flora like a long lost friend. Flora felt instantly at ease as she followed Lily into the large farmhouse kitchen, where Stan was snoring before an open fireplace, showing off the holes in his socks where his feet rested on a tattered leather footstool.

"He insists on that fire, even in summer," Lily whispered, her love for her husband evident in the indulgent look she gave him, "but he works from dawn till dusk, so who am I to refuse him his little pleasures!"

These 'little pleasures' clearly also included a tobacco pipe and a rather large flagon of ale, as both stood atop the day's newspaper on a chipped table next to the man in question.

"Thank you so much for doing this, Lily, it was so kind of you to offer. The other women all looked rather… unapproachable!" Flora accepted the clean apron she was offered.

"It's my pleasure, dearie, and aye, you're right. Though Betty Lafferty is a sweet old dear. Mind you, if you think they're bad, wait till you meet the vicar's wife, she's the worst of the lot!"

"Really?" Flora was keen to encourage the other woman to continue, wanting to know as much about the other ladies in the village as possible.

"Aye, Enid Wright. You can't do right for doing wrong with her," Lily chuckled at her own joke, "she's away visiting her sick mother at the moment, but you'll see. Looks down on the likes of me she does. And fancies herself the best baker in the village – pah!"

"Oh, well, she doesn't sound the friendly sort at all then!" Flora smiled as Lily showed her the large mixing bowl they would be using, and began measuring out the flour. Flora produced the silk-covered notebook she had brought for the purpose of taking notes.

"Oh!" Lily said upon seeing the beautiful item, "Let me get you something to cover that or it'll get ruined!"

They continued two minutes later, once the front cover of Flora's book was safely ensconced in a transparent sandwich bag and Lily was satisfied that none of the mixture would splatter across the delicate material. Whilst the other woman explained each step slowly, Flora found herself relaxing into the experience. They chatted easily about the olden days of the village, as Lily called them, about who had dated whom, who had left the area, the local scandals. Flora let it wash over her as she took careful notes and hoped she could replicate the recipe. Not for the first time, Flora realised that her squinting to see the words she had written was giving her a headache. In her early forties, she refused to accept the time had come to get reading glasses – despite the evidence that she needed them!

They were only interrupted once when Stan produced such a huge snore that he even woke himself up with it. Their old English sheepdog, Bertie, who was snoozing by his owner's feet, jumped into the air, almost as high as Stan, and the two women giggled from the other side of the kitchen. Flora felt a pang of regret and an unwelcome stab of jealousy at the homely scene. She had never had this with her own husband. He had always been either at work or on the golf course. When they did go out together it was to fine dinners or events at the clubhouse, charity balls or holidays abroad with friends. Even then, the men stayed together and the women did their own thing. Flora had never been as lonely as when she was married.

Dragging her mind back to the matter at hand, Flora accepted Lily's offer of a cup of tea while the scones were in the oven. Inevitably, the talk came back to the previous owner of The Rise. Flora shifted uncomfortably in her seat as she listened to how the rent at the farm had been raised just a week before the man's untimely demise, and how Stan had marched up to the manor house to have it out with his landlord. Flora was thankful that Lily didn't enquire as to how she herself came to have taken over the tearoom – feeling slightly guilty at keeping some truth from her new friend, Flora simply invited the couple up for a pot of tea and scone on the house to repay Lily's kindness.

"So, do you bake every day?" Flora asked, thinking wistfully of herself, sprinkled delicately in flour, baking her own goods for the tearoom every morning. It was a lovely daydream.

"No dear, in Baker's Rise it has always been the tradition that the women bake on a certain day of the week. You choose your own day, though. It comes from the old days of our mothers and grandmothers, when they'd do their washing on one day, clean the best parlour another day, then bake on a different one."

"Oh! Well that makes sense! Is your baking day Monday?"

"Not normally, I often do it Saturday like a lot of the women round here do. Quietest day to do it on the farm, what with the farm shop open during the week an' all! I just made an exception for you!"

"Thank you so much, Lily!"

The scones were a picture of perfection as they sat on the cooling rack. Lily made it look so easy, causing Flora to think that perhaps she could bake her own scones after all.

NINE

It was clearly some kind of magic, some secret
ingredient or step in the process that Lily had failed to
divulge, Flora decided miserably as she brought the
batch of flat scones from the new, oversized oven in the
tearoom. Blackened around the edges and still slightly
raw in the middle, they were fit only for the bin. That
was exactly where Flora deposited them, before
turning and sighing at her perfectly pristine, but
achingly empty tearoom. Deciding to close early for the
day, she quickly turned everything off and opted to go
for a walk down into the village. She had spied some
shops that were of interest on her walk up to the farm
last night, and she thought it would do her good to
check them out now. Finding a new outfit and having
her hair done had always perked Flora up in the past,
so she hoped they would do the trick now too. Of
course, the clothes piled up in her sitting room at the

coach house spoke of the fact that a new outfit was the last thing that Flora needed, but she chose to ignore that fact now.

Upon closer inspection, however, Flora had been sorely mistaken. The ladies' boutique, 'Baker's Rise Skirts and Ties,' was clearly stuck in the 1950s and the hairdressers –the predictably named 'Baker's Rise Cuts and Dyes' – stank of the chemicals used in perms and blue rinses. Deflated, Flora pretended to have simply come to hand out fliers for the Tearoom on The Rise and beat a hasty retreat. She had just stepped out of the hair salon, gulping fresh air to help her aching throat and stinging eyes, when Flora bumped into a tall, solid figure. Making a quick apology, she looked up into the startled brown eyes of none other than Phil Drayford.

"Hello Flora! What are you doing in the village at this time of day? School's just finished and I'm taking my marking home for a change."

"Well, I'm doing some marketing, actually," Flora could feel her face blushing red as he scrutinised her features, his eyes twinkling.

"Well, just in time to join me for a quick drink then!" Phil said, linking Flora's arm in his, and turning in the direction of the pub. It felt nice to have some attention, someone who wanted to have a drink with her, so

Flora allowed herself to be led.

The Bun in the Oven was everything you would expect from a quaint British public house – with a dark, wooden bar and furniture, a random selection of local memorabilia on the nicotine-stained walls, and a landlord who looked like he consumed rather a lot of his own products. Daylight was scarce, probably due to the grimy windows which had perhaps deliberately not been cleaned in order to hide the random stains about the place. Flora was happy when Phil guided her into a small corner booth, the only table which afforded any privacy from the rest of the bar, which was surprisingly full for quarter to four on a Tuesday afternoon.

"It's quiz night," Phil whispered, his breath tickling Flora's ear, "they get here as early as they can to get a table and try to get some hints from Ray behind the bar there" – he gestured discreetly with raised eyebrows in the direction of their host – "as to what the questions will be focusing on this week. So they can do some sneaky research on their phones before it starts at five o'clock prompt!"

"Is five o'clock not quite early to be starting?"

"Not in this village! They're mostly in bed by nine!" Little did Phil realise how close to home his joke had hit, as Flora herself had been in bed by nine most nights since arriving. There wasn't much else to do around here than go to bed with a good book. Romances were Flora's favourites, though she realised she may well be trying to fill a hole in her life with the heady fictional relationships she indulged in. Flora could feel herself blushing once again, and fumbled inside her Italian leather handbag for her matching purse, keen to hide her embarrassment.

"Let me pay, Phil…"

"Don't be silly, I invited you! Besides, it's probably best you don't go up to the bar any more often that you absolutely have to."

"Oh? Why is that?"

"You see Ray there?" Phil asked the question in all seriousness, though Flora wondered how anyone could possibly miss the man. With his large jowls and jiggling belly, his ample frame completely filled the space between the back wall of spirits and the large, wooden bar.

"Yes?"

"Well, Ray Dodds is the Casanova of the village!"

"Really? No!" Flora let out an unladylike snort of laughter, and swiftly raised her hand to cover her traitorous mouth.

"Really. I don't know how he does it, but he's the local Lothario! He and old Harold Baker up at your new place used to have bets to see how many notches they could get on their bedposts! And I'm not just talking about their youth," Phil laughed and winked as he walked away to place their drinks order, whilst Flora sat in stunned silence, her hand hiding the huge grin she sported. She would certainly take Phil's advice on board. Attention of that nature – such unwanted attention of that nature, in any case – was best avoided at all costs!

More and more villagers filed in until the whole place was packed. Quiz night was obviously the weekly highlight of the social calendar in these parts. Flora and Phil decided not to join in, but they did order a second and then a third round of drinks, and enjoyed people-watching throughout the competitive event.

"Do you see over at that table to the side of the bar, behind the postie Joe Stanton and his wife?"

Flora tried to peer discretely around Phil, across the room, and behind the odious postman, and saw a very well dressed couple, probably in their fifties.

"Yes, they look rather well-to-do," she whispered.

"Quite. Well, that's Doctor Edwards and his wife Edwina."

"Edwina Edwards?" Flora stifled another snort. This third glass of red wine must be stronger than the others had been, as it was going straight to her head. She no longer cared, as she had an hour ago, that they didn't do Beaujolais or even Shiraz here, simply white wine or red wine. She took another gulp to wash down the laughter that kept threatening to bubble up.

"Yes," Phil smiled back, "he has been the only physician for the village for the past thirty years. Knows everything about everybody, and she works as his secretary at the surgery. Great guard dog she is, won't let anyone in to see him who isn't dying or suffering from impending amputation or paralysis."

"She does look rather scary, that red lipstick is off-putting for a start, and the blue eyeshadow is almost comedic. Has anyone told her the eighties finished a long time ago?" The laugh burst out of Flora before she could suppress it, and she turned her head into Phil's shoulder to muffle the noise. It wasn't her normal nature to be hurtful about others, but the alcohol seemed to remove her filter - one of the reasons Flora's ex-husband had always limited her to two glasses of vino on their nights with friends. One glass when she was anywhere in range of his work colleagues.

"This is the best night out I've had in ages," Phil whispered, his face serious now, his eyes only inches from hers.

Flora straightened and smoothed out her summer dress, composing herself, "Well, that wouldn't be hard around here, would it? I mean, a drink with anyone under forty-five must be an improvement!" They both laughed then, earning them glares from Ray, who took his role as quiz master very seriously.

"Does Ray run the pub alone then? Did none of his dalliances stick?" Flora asked, keen to break the pleasurable tension that was running between them.

"Well, he has been married and divorced five times, but no, he has no lady friend at present as far as I know. His daughter helps him out behind the bar sometimes. He's had a lot of kids, too many to remember, all grown now and left the village, but Shona stuck around. She must be in her twenties, I think, and has a little boy called Aaron who's in my class at school."

Their conversation was interrupted by the pub door slamming open. All assembled paused to stare as a tall, broad man, balding and in about his late fifties entered with a younger woman in a fur coat, who was hanging off his arm. Ray was quick to bring proceedings back under control, and Flora couldn't understand why such an entrance didn't warrant more of an interest. Seeing her still staring at the couple as they walked towards the bar, Phil explained.

"Oh, that's Pat Hughes, local constable, and his new wife Tanya. She's Russian, I think."

"He's the local policeman?" Flora spoke in a stage whisper that would have been heard from across the room had the quiz not still been in full swing, her eyes fixed on the man, who rested the whole top half of his frame on the counter of the bar, as if he couldn't bear the effort of standing up straight.

"Yes, lives in the police force cottage on the Green, which serves as a makeshift station too. Not that we get any crime around here. Just the odd bicycle theft which tuns out to have simply been mislaid, teenagers leaving beer bottles on the cricket club pavilion terrace, that kind of thing. He's got a dog called Frank. Retired police dog, he is, gifted to Pat for thirty years' service in the force, to live out the rest of his canine years in peace. Funny thing is, he's had a more distinguished career than the man himself!"

"Really?"

"Yes, that dog's got a few medals to his name, whereas all Pat's won is the Turnip Competition at the annual vegetable show!"

"His wife is quite the... well, she's making quite the statement!" Flora observed the red stilettos, beneath skin-tight leopard print leggings and a cream jumper which appeared to be adorned by... Flora squinted her eyes to make it out...feathers. Yes, feathers. All topped off by a brown fur coat. Her red lipstick matched that of the doctor's wife, and Flora wondered if the local chemist, 'Baker's Rise Best Buys,' only sold one shade of the lip colour.

It was dark and Flora's legs felt wobbly as they finally left the pub. The quiz had been won by Doctor and Mrs. Edwards – a weekly occurrence, so Phil told her – apparently their competitive streak knew no limit, and they had snatched their winnings of five pounds and thirty-six pence from Ray's sweaty palm before sauntering out. Flora hadn't seen them even order a drink between them.

Ray had given her a leering look as he bade them farewell, and a wink that caused a shudder of revulsion to ripple through Flora. Phil was a gentleman and walked the rather tipsy lady home, before leaving her on her doorstep and going back to his own cottage, on a street named Cook's Row behind the Green. Flora had felt rather bereft as she watched him disappear around the corner of her small driveway, a small part of her wishing a goodnight kiss had been on offer.

TEN

Flora pulled the blankets over her head as the alarm went off for the third time. Her head still spun and the noise from the stupid clock ricocheted through it as if shots had been fired. Flora reached for the glass of water on her bedside table, her mouth was as dry as the Sahara and she licked her lips ineffectually. Four glasses of wine in a woman of almost forty-two should not have this effect, she moaned inwardly, but apparently she was the exception. Gulping down the lukewarm water, Flora sat up, clutching her poor head with her spare hand. The temptation to snuggle back down and not open the tearoom today was so strong, but Flora fought it. She was a professional and had rarely called in sick in the whole of her career, even during that awful time at the start of her marriage to Gregory when they had tried for a family and suffered a string of miscarriages and unsuccessful rounds of

IVF. Gregory had refused to consider adopting, announcing that he would 'have a child from his own loins or none at all.' Flora swallowed down the tears that threatened to rise at the sudden memory. No, she thought resolutely, she would struggle in and manage half a day at least. A strong coffee would set her to rights. *Okay, maybe two cups of coffee.*

The sound of feathers flapping to her side gave Flora a fright, as she turned slowly so as not to set her head off more. Peanut sat there, on the spare pillow next to her, his head cocked at an enquiring angle. Feeling guilty, Flora realised she had not given him much attention recently, and had even forgotten to shut him in his cage at bedtime last night. Perhaps he was better left free to roam, anyway. She had thought last week about maybe bringing him into the shop with her, as a bit of an attraction for families, but would that set bells ringing for the locals? Would they become suspicious if they saw that she was now looking after Harold Baker's pet? Flora decided to think more on it, as she stroked the downy soft feathers on the bird's head and enjoyed the way he nuzzled into her palm. When he wasn't shrieking his name, he was actually quite good company.

"Morning Florence, beautiful day!" Flora was in no mood for the forced humour of Joe Stanton today.

"It's Flora, thank you," she didn't want to play up to it, didn't want to correct him, but something in her wouldn't let the matter lie. It was her name for goodness sakes! Today, of all days, she was not in the mood for the man.

Taking the offered bundle of post, Flora turned on her heel to unlock the door to the tearoom. It was already half past nine. Her bakery goods had sat outside in a cardboard box for nigh on two hours. Flora decided she needed a metal container or something outside for the baker to deposit the goods in every morning. Perhaps she could even trust him with a key, to avoid having to be there so early every day for the delivery? She was thinking about this, as Flora registered that she had not yet heard the tyres of the postal van pulling away.

"Can I help you?" Flora spun around and eyed Joe with her sternest, most impatient look.

"A lot of post you get for the manor house, addressed to you, isn't there?" Flora wanted to wipe the smirk off the man's face. She made a mental note to check each envelope carefully for tampering and then phone the postman's superiors in the closest large town,

Morpeth, to report the invasion of privacy.

"Well, there is no-one in residence, and I am here on the estate, so it makes sense," Flora was severely irked at having to explain herself to the man, so when she turned away this time she marched straight into the shop, slamming the door behind her. Though she did peek out from behind the chintz curtains on the small window to the side of the door, until she was certain he had driven away, before Flora let out the long breath she'd been holding. Perhaps she could get a box for the post, at the bottom of the driveway, to avoid these irritating encounters, she wondered, as she began turning on the lights and machines ready for the day. The big coffee machine, with its arrangement of knobs and buttons that resembled an actual face, sat there as if mocking her, and Flora reluctantly flicked its large, red power switch. Perhaps today would be the day she mastered it.

At half past eleven on the dot, the bell on the tearoom door tinkled to announce Flora's first customer of the day. She herself was wearing an apron covered in drying milk froth and coffee grounds, after an explosive end to that day's attempts at a latte. Patting herself, as if that would suddenly make her pristine again, Flora was surprised and inwardly delighted to see one of the elderly village ladies.

"Good morning. Please take a seat at whichever table you choose!" Flora indicated with her hand the six vacant tables, all bedecked with beautiful vintage crockery, fine lace doilies and a large teapot in the centre.

"Thank you dear, do you serve elevenses?" The woman hovered just in the doorway, as if she wasn't yet sure whether she was going to stay or not.

"I certainly do, with cream scones, or crumpets, teacakes or banana loaf. Or a lovely Victoria sponge if you fancy!"

The older woman's face lit up, "Ooh, I do like a slice of Victoria sponge," she looked as if she were about to sit down at the table nearest the counter until a thought suddenly struck her, "you didn't make it yourself, did you dear?"

Flora sucked in a breath between her teeth, the woman having unwittingly touched a nerve, "No, indeed, only the finest from the local baker."

"Perfect, I'll give it a go," she said rather seriously, as if she was committing herself to a monthly contract and not simply tea and cake. Her rheumy eyes looked Flora up and down, not just at the splattered apron, but also at the tailored suit trousers and crisp blouse. Flora decided inwardly that she should try to dress the part of a local from now on. Her city clothes were at odds with the country lifestyle she was now aspiring to fit in with. Clearly, she did not look like someone who was good at baking. And she desperately wanted to have the aura of an accomplished cake maker.

Flora felt the pressure begin to rise as she stood patiently waiting to take the lady's order. It was imperative that she make a good impression on potential regular village customers like this one. It was the only way she would build up regular business that wasn't the occasional tourist, lost in the wilds of the Northumberland National Park.

"I'm Flora, Flora Miller," she said, to break the uncomfortable silence as the woman took out her spectacles, affixed them to the tip of her nose, and began perusing the menu. Her tut tutting and slight shaking of the head were all noticed by Flora, who was on tenterhooks by the time the lady actually spoke.

"Pleased to meet you, Flora, I'm Betty. Betty Lafferty. Former chairwoman of the local Women's Institute. I only stepped down at last year's fete to give someone else a chance at the role. After all, I had held the title for fifteen years. I still won Best Scone at last year's fayre though, so I haven't lost my touch," she laughed lightly, as Flora felt a ball of concrete settle in the pit of her stomach. She had no hope of impressing such an esteemed baker as this. Not with shop-bought goods that weren't even home-made. It was over before it had a chance to begin, and Flora's shoulders slumped in defeat.

"Now dear, don't you be downhearted just because I'm famous in the local area for my baking. Just you do your best," Betty added. Normally, Flora would have been immediately irritated by the condescending tone, but in this instance she was simply grateful to be given a glimmer of hope. Perhaps if she buttered Betty up, she might get a lesson or two. Perhaps even an invite to join the hallowed institution that was the W.I.

"Do you know who owns the big house now, The Rise?" Betty asked around a mouthful of Victoria sponge. She had invited Flora to join her at the table, there being no other customers, and the two were sharing a huge pot of Earl Grey tea. Betty had already quizzed Flora on her marital status, where she had come from, and whether she planned to join the village fete committee. Flora had responded that she would be honoured to help in any way she could, even though secretly, the thought of joining a group of formidable women, plus the vicar, on a committee to arrange the highlight of the village calendar, filled her with dread.

"Well, ah," Flora tripped over her reply, eventually just sitting looking non-committal.

"It's just, the lord of the manor, so to speak, usually judges the cake competitions at the fete," Betty continued, seemingly unaware of Flora's discomfort, "who will decide on Best Scone and Spongiest Sponge now, I wonder?" Her wrinkled face scrunched up in deep thought as she eyed Flora from over the huge piece of cake which was raised to her mouth.

"I'm not sure, the vicar perhaps?" Flora tried to be helpful.

"Pah, that idiot wouldn't know his cranberries from his cherries!" Betty scoffed, "All that matters to him is that stupid roof. Besides, it's his wife Enid who normally wins the Best Scone competition. Right put out she was last year when I snuck past her to first place. Should've seen her black look when Harold Baker gave me a peck on the cheek as he handed me the rosette," Betty paused as a blush crept up her wobbling chins. "It would be a conflict of interests for the vicar to judge the scones."

Flora had no idea who would take Harold's role in the village event, but she didn't voice her thoughts. There was at least another month till the big fete, so perhaps things would be clearer by then.

Betty left, her face a picture of delight when Flora said she could have her elevenses on the house, promising to come back another Tuesday with some friends. *You have to speculate to accumulate,* thought Flora resignedly, as she contemplated another day with no income. *Small steps, one day at a time,* her new mantra, on repeat in her head as Flora finished cleaning the coffee machine from its earlier outburst and decided to spend the afternoon up at the manor house, hopefully making some noticeable progress there. Everything in Baker's Rise seemed to go at a snail's pace, from its slovenly policeman to the shops stuck in a time warp. Quite the opposite to the rat race she was used to, and in a lot of ways Flora was thankful for that fact. She knew she needed to adjust her sails. Perhaps find a hobby to occupy her until she could perfect the baking. Thoughts of potential distractions flooded Flora's mind – top of the list, writing the novel she had always promised herself she would – as she nipped back to the coach house to collect Peanut, before making her way up to the main house with him on her shoulder.

ELEVEN

Flora pulled open the dusty, once-green velvet curtains in the once-grand study and sneezed twice as the tiny particles flew around her. Peanut had flown straight to the sitting room when they arrived, and Flora decided to leave him to it. He clearly used to have his cage in that room, and felt an affinity for it, so Flora was happy to leave him to it. She could hear him screeching, "Peanut! Peanut! Peanut!" and so closed the heavy oak door to shut out the sound.

Today, Flora was on a mission. Reverend Wright had mentioned that the tearoom used to give half its proceeds to the church. Flora wanted to find a clue as to why the tearoom had been closed. She also wanted to know where all of the money from rents had gone. The villagers assumed Harold had been rolling in it, and Flora knew that was not the case. Quite the opposite in fact. Apart from the state of disrepair which this house was in, Harry Bentley had shown her Harold Baker's bank accounts. A sad state of affairs all round.

Flora decided to abandon the pile of papers which she had been going through on previous visits, which seemed mainly to be internet receipts for parrot food and golf paraphernalia. Instead, she opted to focus her efforts on a pile which rose up from the seat of the desk chair, towering above her like the leaning tower of Pisa, as if it might collapse at any moment. Indeed, Flora thought it was probably defying the laws of gravity for having stayed upright so long. She reached up on tiptoes to take the first quarter of the large stack, but in doing so lost her balance. The papers fell to the floor, scattering all around her like a sudden snow storm, and Flora herself staggered backwards until she was halted when her foot landed in something wet. The bucket full of water, which must have been placed under a leak in the roof, as evidenced by the brown, bulging damp patch on the cream ceiling above, tipped as if in slow motion. Flora yanked her sodden foot out, muttering under her breath at another pair of beautiful Italian shoes ruined, as the bucket tipped over completely, depositing its murky contents over the filthy, fraying rug which sat under the desk.

"The papers!" Flora shrieked, coming suddenly to her senses and getting her priorities in order. She grabbed a dusty throw from a large green sofa, which sat under the bay window facing the back garden, and sneezed as she threw it over the puddle. Thankfully, most of the papers had missed the deluge, and those that were sodden seemed to only include gardening catalogues and rifle adverts. Nevertheless, leaving the throw over the wet patch, Flora rushed into the hallway, where she had previously spotted a huge storage cupboard built underneath the majestic staircase. Flinging it open, Flora was assailed by the stench of chemicals and small animals. Praying that there were no mice or, heaven forbid, rats, and holding her nose, she ventured further in. About to grab a filthy mop and cloth which she saw standing against the wall, something on the shelf ahead caught Flora's eye. It was a battered, navy blue box, with holes in the corners of the cardboard and the writing on the top almost illegible. The picture on the front, however, was clear – a typewriter.

Excitement fluttered in Flora's belly like butterflies, as she dropped the mop and reached on tiptoe once again to get the box from the shelf. It was heavy and her knees almost buckled, so that Flora steadied herself against the cupboard doorframe, from where she could lower the box to the ground in the hallway. Her anticipation was great as Flora opened the box, praying that she wouldn't find some rusty tools or more unused cleaning products. Inside, sat a beautiful vintage typewriter in mint condition. Flora drank in the sight of it. Since she was a girl, she had always fancied herself a writer, in the mould of Barbara Cartland or Danielle Steel, setting pulses racing and hearts aflutter with her words. Perhaps, Flora thought almost giddy with excitement, this was the universe telling her now was the time! Inside the box were a number of unused ink ribbons and an instruction booklet. Her watery woes forgotten, Flora lifted the machine out, shocked by its heavy weight, and gingerly ran her fingers over the keys before putting it carefully on the floor at her feet. This was a sign indeed.

"All okay?" The male voice caused Flora to jump a few feet in the air from fright. She turned her head sharply, pulling the muscle in her neck, to see an ancient, grizzly looking man poking his head around the side door which she always used to access the house. "I didn't mean to frighten ye lass, I just saw you come in earlier when I was tending to the roses."

"The roses?" Flora tried to rein in her addled senses.

"Aye, Mr. Baker liked them looking at once a fortnight in the summer months."

"I'm sorry but he is, ah, deceased," it was turning into a very strange conversation, Flora thought, "has been for ten months!"

"Aye, I know that lass," he spoke slowly now as if she were stupid, "and I know there's no pay, but I've been doing it these past twenty years, since I retired. Used to have a good natter with young Harold too, over a cuppa like."

"Oh, I see, I'm afraid I don't have a kettle up here!" Flora wondered if he was angling for a drink, before regretting her harsh tone. Perhaps this man could fill in some of the gaps in her knowledge about the former resident of The Rise? "I do run the new Tearoom on The Rise, though," she added quickly, "perhaps you'd like to call in tomorrow morning… on the house?"

"Oh, well, if you're offering! William Northcote," he ventured further into the dimly lit hallway and offered Flora a grubby hand, "everyone calls me Billy."

"Pleased to meet you, Billy," Flora would have preferred it if he'd removed the filthy gardening glove before politely making her acquaintance, but she shook it briefly out of courtesy. "If you pop in about ten tomorrow?"

"Perfect, lass. And will there be chocolate cake?"

"I, ah, well, yes," Flora had found that with the villagers it was almost always better to comply. They always persuaded you in the end anyway.

Billy beat a hasty retreat, apparently he had a lot more dead-heading to do before the day was over. Flora wondered if she should ask Harry Bentley to start paying the man. She made a mental note to add it to the to-do list which was affixed by a magnet to her fridge in the coach house. She was desperate to fiddle with the typewriter, but reluctantly put it back in its box. It would have to wait until she got home – a reward of sorts for several hours sorting through papers, which she must begin now.

Avoiding the huge wet patch, which had brought all sorts of worrying-looking gunk up from the rug, Flora concentrated on the papers which had fallen on the dry side of the desk. Receipts, prescriptions, bank statements... all were dealt with and placed in the correct spot under Flora's quick fingers. She had a bag for shredding, a bag for recycling, and a pile to be filed in the large filing cabinet against the wall which, ironically, itself held very few papers and was only a quarter full. It had evidently been too much effort for Harold to move the opened post into the cabinet.

Just as she was about to stop for the day, her legs cramping where she knelt on them, her eyes sore from squinting and she herself feeling desperate for a coffee, a sheet of a paper caught Flora's eye. Lying by itself just out of range of the ones she had been sorting, it stood out because it was so stark. No bright logo, no shiny advertising. It was a simply white sheet, with black mis-matched lettering. Leaning on her knees so that she could reach it, Flora squinted to make sure she was reading the single sentence correctly.

You know what you did, and you will pay the price

The letters had been cut from newspaper, which was now turning slightly yellow, and stuck onto the plain white sheet of paper. Flora felt a sickness in her stomach. Where earlier she had felt excitement from one discovery, she now felt dread from another. This was clearly a threat, how else could it be interpreted? Flora carefully put the sheaf of paper inside the box with the typewriter. She doubted any fingerprints could be found on it after this time – how long she didn't even know, it could be years old, though the yellowing of the newspaper was only feint which suggested the message had been created not too long ago. She would have to take it to Pat Hughes, though Flora had no desire whatsoever to deal with the local policeman. She knew she was being judgemental, having never talked to him personally, but from what she'd learnt in the pub, he didn't take his job too seriously. Perhaps Phil would come with her? Flora decided to text him this evening.

After the shock from Billy and now this, Flora's nerves were shredded. She stood up on shaking legs, her muscles protesting at the change in position, and picked up the heavy typewriter box. She was halfway to the side door, when Flora remembered her feathery friend.

"Peanut! Peanut, come here!" she called, but no sound came. Grumbling, Flora lowered the typewriter to the floor and trudged along the corridor to the sitting room at the front of the house. There, sitting on the otherwise empty coffee table with his head tucked into his wings and apparently fast asleep, sat the parrot. It was such a sweet sight, that Flora moved her hand to stroke him. Sensing her presence, the bird's eyes flew open and he looked straight down to his feet, clutching the crumb from the other day with his claws, then back up to Flora as he shrieked "Peanut" at a rate of several decibels.

Flora stepped back from the force of it, annoyed that she had felt moved by the sight of the animal. Evidently, he had screeched himself to exhausted sleep whilst she'd been busy, but was now making up for lost time.

"Do be quiet!" Flora said sternly as she turned on her heel and left the room. She had collected the typewriter and was almost out of the building before she heard the swoop of his wings as her new pet followed her.

TWELVE

Flora was exhausted by the time she lugged the heavy box down the hill, Peanut perched on the top like a mast. She staggered into the coach house and lowered the typewriter gently onto the tiny kitchen table, before putting the kettle on. The thought of the worrisome message, hidden for now inside the box, niggled at her, and Flora wondered who could have sent it. Certainly, there was no shortage of suspects from what she had already been told from the villagers, and she hadn't even met everyone yet! If whoever sent the note was serious, then Harold was almost lucky that he had died of a tragic accident before someone offed him. Besides, Flora thought, she hadn't been through even half of the paperwork. There could well be more threats. How long had Harold been receiving them before his death?

Phil had said he'd been a lady's man, so had he broken another heart? Even in his seventies, as he was? Or was it something, or rather someone, from his past come back to torment him. Add to that the rent increases year on year, how he'd apparently bled the village dry, Flora thought it would probably be quicker to list the people who'd actually liked the man. At the moment, that amounted to Harry Bentley – though that was more a professional relationship – and the man from today, the gardener, what was his name? Ah yes, William Northcote. Flora mulled it over as she sipped at her coffee, pulling a face as all she had here was instant granules. She grabbed her phone from her handbag and texted Phil, asking him if he'd fancy coming round for dinner. She hoped he could perhaps explain the message in a non-threatening light, though Flora could not think of any angle which could describe it that way. She knew in her gut that she had a responsibility to show it to the local policeman, but what harm would one more day do? The man concerned was dead anyway.

Peanut had seemed withdrawn since they returned, so Flora fussed over him, playing with the bells attached to his perch and offering him a new treat to gnaw on. He had willingly gone inside his cage, which was not a normal occurrence. No amount of cajoling would change the parrot's mood, so Flora eventually gave up when a text came back from Phil saying that he would love to come for a meal, but could they make it Wednesday night as he had a parent and teacher meeting today. Replying with a time for the following evening, Flora was shocked when a shrill ringing filled the small room. Not Peanut's antics, this time, Flora eventually located the source as an ancient landline telephone on a windowsill well hidden behind a curtain. Flora hadn't even been aware she was paying for a telephone line, so used was she to using her mobile phone, and made a mental note to get it disconnected. For now, though, she looked at the item warily, as the annoying ringing did not cease. Clearly, whoever wanted to contact her was desperate.

"Hello?" Flora almost whispered the word, as if the receiver might reach out and bite her.

"Good Evening, Ms. Miller I presume?" A haughty voice on the other end enquired.

"Ah, yes, to whom am I speaking?"

"This is Enid Wright. Wife to the Vicar of the parish. We have not yet been acquainted."

"No, quite so, ah, hello Enid."

"Most parishioners refer to me as Mrs. Wright."

"Do they?" this was exasperating, and Flora was tired.

"They do. Anyway, I was not here to welcome you to the village. Family matters called me away. We'll see you at the vicarage tomorrow for an early supper at six."

"Tomorrow? I'm afraid I already have plans."

"Better plans than a meal with your local clergy, shepherd of our village flock?"

"Well, ah not better, just already made before you called. I could do…" Flora desperately tried to think of any excuses to postpone the event, before reluctantly settling on "Friday perhaps?"

"No, it will have to be Thursday then, as the Parish council meets every first Friday in the month at seven o'clock prompt and I am required to make the cups of tea. I assume you have no plans for Thursday?" This last was said in such a disdainful tone, that Flora had the petulant thought that she might just hang up and claim a fault on the line.

An annoying inability to break the rules prevented her from doing so, however, and instead she simply said, "Thursday at six will be fine."

"Very well, don't be late to the vicarage," and the
woman herself rang off the line, leaving a stunned
Flora not knowing quite what had hit her.

With no dinner companion, and a sulking parrot, Flora
made herself a cheese and ham toastie with a bit of
coleslaw and salad on the side, before settling into her
favourite armchair with her notebook and pen. The
typewriter remained in its box – not because Flora
didn't desperately want to get it out, rather because
she felt spooked by the message which rested
alongside it. She had decided to unbox them both
when Phil came the following evening. For now,
though, Flora made some notes about everyone she
had met, things they had mentioned in passing about
the deceased Harold Baker, and any family
connections in the village. As was common in this area
of rural Northumberland, people often not only knew
each other's business, but they had actual blood ties to
it. Phil had whispered in the pub that it was rumoured
there was some distant family connection between
Doctor Edwards and the pub landlord, Ray Dodds,
though the doctor would never admit to the fact that
they were second cousins. Flora could see no family
resemblance so she decided the link must be tenuous at
best.

It kept her mind occupied for a while, wondering how a man as disliked as Harold could possibly have stayed in the small village for his whole life. But, she surmised, he owned the village so why on earth would he leave? Having never married, despite his wayward youth and many liaisons since, nor had children, Harold was a bit of a mystery to her – a mystery which Flora intended to solve. She loved a good puzzle.

Eventually turning her thoughts from him, Flora started a fresh, blank page and began making an outline for the plot of her first novel. It would be a grand affair about…well, a grand affair. Her first book would be sure to sell hundreds of thousands of copies. Flora daydreamed about being able to hire someone – someone with great baking skills at that – to run the tearoom, whilst she went on book tours in hot, beautiful places. Perhaps the delightful Phil would accompany her…

Before she realised it, it was time for Flora to settle down for the night. The tearoom awaited early the next day, and she was still exhausted from her hangover. Flora felt a bit melancholy that the shine had worn off the tearoom project for her now. Reality had well and truly sunk in, and she wondered if she would be able to do it day in and day out, talking to herself in an empty café and fighting a great, steaming machine.

Best get onto that novel quick, Flora thought, as she heard the flutter of feathers land on the pillow beside her and nuzzle into her neck as she drifted off to sleep.

THIRTEEN

"Morning Freda!"

"It's Flora," the usual morning greetings were exchanged with the exasperating postman as Flora arrived, just in time for opening. She had spent time 'dressing down' for the day, keen to appear approachable for her chat with Billy. How in her past life she had managed to get into the City before eight every morning, and after an hour-long commute too, she had no idea. Perhaps it was village life rubbing off on her or, worse still, the start of middle age. Flora suppressed a shudder at the thought and began her morning chores. She had reduced the order from the baker, just temporarily until she had more customers, to save her from eating the cakes which would go out of date otherwise. Flora was saddened to weigh herself that morning to find that she had put on seven pounds since moving into the coach house and no doubt eating the bakery goods was mostly to blame. It simply would not do if she couldn't fit into her tailored dresses for Christmas festivities. Those events were still some five months away, and pointless worrying about now, however. So, Flora took in her half-order of cakes and scones with sagging shoulders and a drooping mouth, feeling rather sad and defeated about the whole tearoom venture.

Ten o'clock arrived and there was no sign of Billy Northcote. Flora felt her spirits sag even further and was feeling very sorry for herself. She hadn't even turned on the monster coffee machine yet, as she was sure no-one would want one anyway. A defeatist attitude, she knew, but Flora couldn't help it. The melancholy cloud and a huge wave of loneliness left her feeling quite bereft. She had been so busy since moving here that she'd had very little time to contemplate either her marriage breakdown – though that was a relief really and a long time in the making – or her new situation. She was just thinking of popping home to see Peanut and enjoying his company for a quick half hour, when the bell on the door rang and Billy popped his head around.

"Sorry I'm late lass, had to set up the bowling green for

a match this afternoon. Big league game with the Witherham lot. Have you got space for me now?"

Flora looked around at the empty tables ruefully. She had swapped the cups and saucers around today to mix things up a bit. It had been the highlight of her morning so far.

"Of course, Billy, I've been looking forward to your visit!"

"Oh, thank you kindly," he said as he came in and chose the table closest to the door. His eyebrows raised imperceptibly at the array of fine china and pristine doily and cotton tablecloth as he looked down at his work-soiled clothes, but Flora brushed over his discomfort.

"Do you like the crockery? I found it all…" she suddenly realised she was about to say 'at the mansion house' so instead finished her sentence with, "in charity shops. Can you believe it?" The man seemed to relax a little, thinking he wasn't dealing with family heirlooms, and Flora pottered behind the counter preparing his slice of chocolate cake and English Breakfast tea. She made a pot for two, as she had with Betty Lafferty, and sat down opposite her guest. He looked even more ancient in the morning light which was spilling into the stone building. A few select walls were still the scrubbed, bare stone – which Flora had thought would be a lovely original touch – but most of the others had been plastered and painted a pretty lemony yellow which currently enhanced the sun's glow into the room. Billy's wizened face broke into a gummy grin, which revealed that at least half of his teeth were missing.

"You can ask lass, don't be shy!"

Flora blushed, "Ah, how old are you, Billy?"

"Ninety-one and a half," he declared proudly, "and still fit as a fiddle!"

"No! I wouldn't have put you at a day over eighty," Flora replied politely, "you certainly seem very spritely! And you've been gardening at The Rise for twenty years, you say?" she tried to lead into the discussion subtly. About as subtle as a brick, really.

"Well, twenty years since I retired and have been doing the rose garden at the back for free. Before that, I were the head gardener for the whole estate and got paid for my efforts."

"Wow, so you've been working here for…"

"Sixty-three years," he looked like he was doing the mental calculation in his head, and Flora sat patiently, astounded.

"But you've not been paid for twenty years?" she couldn't help herself. The whole notion of him working for Harold for free seemed a bit... well, far-fetched.

"Nope, just a bottle of beer every Christmas. I love that rose garden though. That and the bowls, keeps me fit and young!"

"Quite! And you enjoyed your chats with Harold then?"

"Yes, he was likeable enough. Of course, I knew him since he was a young 'un. He always lived in that house. First with his parents, then when they scarpered off to retire in Portugal, he took over running the place. Plenty of women in and out over the years, but none stuck. He wasn't liked by the locals in general, but he was always good to me. Always praised the roses, he did," Flora silently thought that Harold would of course have praised Billy's work, if only to continue getting it for free, but she bit her tongue.

"Was he not lonely in that big house by himself then?"

Billy wolfed down the chocolate cake in three huge mouthfuls, small crumbs attached to his rough, white stubble the only evidence that it had even existed. He looked hopefully from his plate, across to Flora, and then back to the plate again, before she took the hint and stood up to fetch him another slice. Flora continued to listen to his chat as she moved behind the counter.

"Aye, I reckon so. Must've been very lonely, else why would he pass the time of day with an old man like me?" Billy chuckled to himself, "Seriously though, he had plenty of visitors, just not many that were very welcome, if you know what I mean."

"Oh?" Flora returned to her seat, wishing woefully that she had got herself a piece of cake too.

"Yup, they were always storming up there, the village folk. Rents too high, or him not keeping to his landlord duties of repairs and such. Then that awful pious bloke, you know the vicarage one, up every other day demanding money for the roof, that he open the tearoom, and all that. I got the impression Harold just closed the tearoom to spite the man!"

"Really?" Flora turned the word into a question in the hope of keeping Billy talking.

"Aye," she needn't have worried, he was in his full flow now, "why, even the day he died he had three visitors that very morning. I was doing the pruning round the front, just as an extra favour like, and was bent down behind the bushes, but I heard them comin' up the drive I did. I know which day he died, you see, because it was me as found him late in the afternoon, when I popped in with the new Charles Rose catalogue. I must have fallen asleep for my afternoon nap on a garden bench so it were later in the day by the time I went up to the house for a cuppa. And there he were, collapsed, his face all… well you won't be wanting to hear about that, a fine lady like yerself."

"Oh my goodness, you must have had quite the shock. And him, rest his soul. But there were three visitors, you say?"

"Aye, first there was that schoolteacher. Tall bloke, about your age. Arrived just as I was getting started."

"Phil Drayford?" Flora tried to ignore the sinking feeling that filled her abdomen.

"Aye. Then there was Houghton. I'd know that farmer's wellies anywhere. I popped my face up above the hedge and that man had a face on him like there was hell to pay for something. Then, lots of shouting I heard, 'You'll pay for this!' and the like! And just as he were leaving she arrived."

"She?"

"Aye, it were definitely a woman, as she was wearing those clip-cloppy shoes the fancy ones wear – like yours!" he looked down pointedly at Flora's heels. She had opted for a very understated dress of light grey denim, but couldn't resist a pair of mauve heels to set it off.

"Indeed, and did you see anything else of her?"

"Nay lass, I don't bother meself with women nowadays, but I smelt her, like a fine summer day she were, one that was drenched in something sickly sweet. Like she'd put on a nice scent but used the whole bottle."

"Really?"

"Aye, reminded me of the constable's woman – you know, the Polish one?"

"Oh, I thought she was Russian?" Flora tried to keep up with the jump in conversation.

"Polish, like from Poland," it was like a switch had been flicked in his mind, "I was still a lad when war broke out, you know. Even here in the countryside we had the Anderson shelters and then the evacuees started arriving from Newcastle. That's how I met the beautiful girl who would eventually become my wife…" his eyes glazed over as Billy was lost in memories and Flora sat and listened contentedly, wondering if she'd ever have a true love story like that to recount, or if she would end up as lonely as she felt right now.

FOURTEEN

By the time Billy left after a fresh pot of tea and a scone
with jam and clotted cream, Flora was feeling lonelier
than ever. He had led a long and mostly happy life
until he was widowed some six years earlier,
something which sent a pang of yearning and even
jealousy through Flora. It seemed that since then Billy
himself had shared the same loneliness that Flora now
felt. She had invited him to pop in whenever he was
passing, having enjoyed his company – and not just for
the tidbits of information.

Flora resisted the croissants which needed eating and
were calling to her like a siren's song, and instead had
two rice cakes which she had deliberately brought
from home for her lunch. She decided to stay until two
o'clock and then lock up and stop in to say hello to

Peanut before taking her car into Morpeth to buy
something lovely for her meal with Phil that evening.
There was a Marks and Spencer Food shop there, so
Flora knew she could buy a beautiful ready-made meal
and fresh starter that would pass as home-made!
Perhaps she should add cookery to her baking lessons?
That reminded her, she needed to phone Lily and
arrange another scone lesson...

All of this and more was whirring around Flora's head,
so she didn't hear Harry's car approach until she heard
the door bang as he climbed out.

"Afternoon Flora," he said as he entered the café, his
cheerful smile forcing Flora to smile in return. She
always found the older man's company a source of
reassurance and welcomed his visits to the tearoom.

"Harry! What a lovely surprise. Can I get you
anything?"

"No my dear, just a flying visit to check that all is
going well. Have you made any progress up at the big
house?"

Flora spoke in gushing terms of the typewriter, and
desperately wanted to mention the sinister note, but
felt it was better if as few people as possible knew
about that before she took it to the police. She would

just tell Phil this evening and no-one else. Instead, she spoke of the mountains of papers still to sort.

"Ah well, you'll get there in the end! How's this little business going?"

Flora felt her stomach drop as she had to admit that things were not going well. Not going well at all, in fact.

"Give it some time, it's been less than a week since you opened," Harry seemed to have a confidence which Flora did not share, but she nodded politely.

They were interrupted by the tinkling of the door announcing another customer and Betty Lafferty breezed in, her rain hat tied in a bow under her chin leaving only a few stray, grey curls to poke out. Glancing out of the window, Flora saw that a heavy drizzle had begun to spoil the pleasant summer's day. Upon seeing Harry, Betty appeared to freeze in the doorway, looking flustered and blushing a bright shade of red.

"Betty!" Harry said with gusto, offering her his arm and leading her to a table in the far corner, "I've just arrived myself. Shall we share a pot?" Apparently the 'flying visit' has been replaced with a lingering lunch, Flora noted happily as she busied herself making tea and sandwiches. It was like hosting a pair of teenagers, the giggles and whispers that were coming from that end of the room. It was apparent that, not only did the couple share more than a passing acquaintance and had clearly done so for some long while, but they were also actually...yes, they were actually flirting with one another!

Flora couldn't hide her smile as she brought them their food. She declined their polite offer that she join the table, and instead retreated to her counter, deliberately turning on the coffee machine so that the bursts of steam and chugging noises would give the couple some privacy.

It was an hour or so later when Harry paid the whole bill and took his leave of both women. Her legs aching, Flora joined Betty at the table with a fresh pot of tea. It became quickly apparent that Betty had called by for a second day running in the hope of getting a 'pensioners' discount' that she argued each shop in the village offered – half price for all the over-65s on a Wednesday. Flora had never heard of it, but given the quirky nature of the village it was certainly quite possibly true. As it was, Harry had paid for Betty's share too, so Flora simply said that this fresh cup of tea was on the house.

Betty's eyes were still shining from her quasi-amorous encounter, and Flora desperately wanted to quiz the older woman on whether anything was, had been, or would ever happen between her and Harry, but it was far too personal a question for a septuagenarian whom Flora had only met the day before. Instead, they chatted about the village fete, cake making, the delights of London, and whether it would be a freezing winter. As much as Flora enjoyed the company, she couldn't help but keep checking her watch to see if she still had time to make it into M&S in Morpeth. Eventually, Betty rose to leave, but only when even the very dregs of the pot of tea had been drunk and Flora had promised to go for Sunday lunch after church that week.

FIFTEEN

It was two hours later when a drenched, irritable and exhausted Flora finally pushed open the front door of the coach house. She wrangled her bags into the house and through to the kitchen counter feeling awful that Peanut had been alone for so long. She had already decided on her drive back from town that the bird would come into the tearoom with her every day from now on. He flew straight to her shoulder, nuzzling Flora's ear in greeting and she was glad there was at least someone there to welcome her back.

Checking the old clock on the kitchen wall propelled Flora into further action. First she had been delayed by Betty, then by temporary traffic lights on the main road after the village – though there were no workmen in sight – then Flora had spent time in Marks and

Spencer's deliberating whether the dinner warranted a candle or two. Would it seem like she was setting things up for romance? In the end, she had decided against it. Unfortunately, it meant that she was now left with only thirty-five minutes to shove the lasagna in the oven, prepare a Greek salad, put the ingredients together for a salmon pâté starter, and shower and change. She wished she had had the forethought to choose her outfit earlier in the day, but alas that was not the case. It would have to be a 'whatever comes out of the wardrobe first' job!

As a result, Flora was rather overdressed in a 1920s cocktail-style black chiffon dress and still drying her hair when the doorbell rang. At first she did not hear it, until a sharp rap on the kitchen window caught her attention where she stood in the back hallway. Flora's heart jumped to her mouth in fright, though she had not been given any reason since arriving in the village to think this was not a safe area. *Too long living in London,* she thought to herself, feeling silly that her heart was beating fast in her chest and her face a ghastly shade of white when she opened the door to Phil. She really wished she'd had time to curl her straight hair a little and to apply some mascara and blusher. Flora had always been told that her eyes were one of her best features – neither blue nor grey they were a beautiful mixture of both. Unfortunately, her eyelids had become slightly saggy with age, and Flora would have felt much more comfortable with a small bit of make-up to enhance her features!

Flora invited Phil into the small sitting room and offered him a drink, muttering an embarrassed explanation as to why she wasn't quite ready yet and why he had to move a selection of dresses before he could take a seat, before rushing back to dry the last half of her hair. It was when she turned off the hairdryer for the second time, that Flora heard the parrot. The sound of wings flapping in annoyance and his shrieks of 'Peanut' could be heard through even the thick stone walls of the cottage. Flora rushed back into the sitting room, where Peanut was circling Phil's head, slapping his cheeks and scalp with his wings and screeching the same word on repeat. Flora felt mortified. She'd never seen the bird in such a tizz.

"Peanut, Peanut, cage now!" Flora shouted, to no avail. It took her physically reaching out to grab the bird with both hands and cuddling him to her chest, shushing him and stroking his yellow head feathers before the parrot would even begin to calm down.

"I didn't know you had Reggie?" Phil commented when they could both hear themselves think again.

"Who's Reggie?" Flora was confused. Her head was thumping with the start of a migraine, and she'd suddenly remembered that she'd left the M&S empty food packets strewn over the kitchen bench. She hoped Phil hadn't noticed as he'd looked in the window, that being the closest to the driveway.

"The parrot, Reggie, I didn't know you had him."

"Oh, yes, he, ah, well he came with the house... with the job... at the tearoom," Flora stumbled over the words. She felt awful, lying by omission. Perhaps she should confide in Phil, just him and not the whole village, but she wanted to talk that through with Harry Bentley before she said anything. He would know the teacher better than she did and of course his judgement wouldn't be clouded by the man's handsome features as hers was! Flora was so busy trying to explain – or avoid explaining – how she came by the bird, that the most important fact of the conversation almost passed her by.

"Sorry, Phil, did you say Reggie? I'm sure his name is Peanut. It's the only word he says and he squawks it almost constantly!"

"It's definitely Reggie, I think. I saw him every time I visited The Rise, he was always in the main reception room, and Harold always called him Reggie! Besides, he was saying full sentences back then. Had a huge vocabulary. That parrot always hated me, after the first time I visited and it landed on my leg. I was wearing running shorts and his claws dug in so I shooed him off – he's had it in for me ever since. Looks like the same bird, but are you sure it is?"

Flora chewed on the inside of her cheek, perplexed, "Well, Harry said it was Mr. Baker's parrot," she replied quietly, feeling unsure of herself now, "but they sound like such different birds."

"Only one way to tell," Phil said, his forehead wrinkled in thought, "you go into the kitchen and call 'Reggie' and see if he comes to you."

It seemed a sensible test, so that was exactly what Flora did. Within seconds, the bird had left his perch and come to join her in the other room, landing effortlessly on her outstretched arm.

"Well I never!" Flora almost couldn't believe it, "Why would he say 'peanut' so often then? And nothing else at all?" It was a riddle indeed, though clearly not one Phil wanted to participate in solving, as he swiftly changed the subject to his day at school, handing his hostess the bottle of wine he had brought. Flora, desperate as she was to discuss the subject of Reggie further, was distracted by the smoke alarm going off in the kitchen and rushed to save the lasagna. She only hoped as she did so, that the whole evening was salvageable too.

SIXTEEN

The food eaten, Flora realised with dismay that she had forgotten to buy a dessert. She could have really done with a sugar hit right now, as conversation over the meal had seemed stilted and strained. They had opened the bottle of red wine which Phil had brought and had half a glass each, but Phil had said that as he had school tomorrow he would not drink any more. Flora felt so self-conscious at the idea of drinking by herself, that she hadn't yet plucked up the courage to pour herself another glass. In the end, Phil took the decision out of her hands, by topping up Flora's glass as they moved to have a more comfortable seat on the sofa.

"So, what brings you to Baker's Rise, then? Wouldn't be my first choice of destination after the lights of

London!" Phil chuckled. He had a small dimple just below his right cheek which came out when he smiled, and Flora thought it very attractive. She tried hard not to stare and instead took a gulp of wine.

"Well, ah, I'm very recently divorced. I was looking for a new place to live after the marital home and then I... saw the tearoom opportunity here. I was desperate for a slower pace of life, some country air, a new start really."

"Well, it's definitely slow around here!" Phil joked. His mood seemed to have improved now they were not talking about either the bird or their neighbours.

"And you?" Flora enquired, "What brought you to teach in such a small school?" She regretted the question as soon as she had asked it, as Phil's mouth turned down and he assumed his distant air once again.

"Well, my dad lived here, in Baker's Rise, moved here when he retired. I lived in Alnwick and taught in a large primary school there, until three years ago when he was diagnosed with Alzheimer's disease. He didn't ask me to, but I wanted to look after him. My mother died five years ago – cancer. I've got no siblings," his voice was flat and devoid of emotion.

"I'm so sorry. Is he..?"

"Yes, he passed eleven months ago now. The cottage I rent was his. I don't know why I stayed in the village really, except that there is only one other teacher at the school and I don't want to drop them in it. I also inherited my dad's cat, Champion. It's hard to find rentals in Alnwick that accept pets, so..." he trailed off, seemingly deep in thought. Flora wanted to ask him about his cottage, if he rented it from the Baker estate, though she was pretty sure she knew the answer to that. She wondered how the price rises instigated regularly by Harold had affected his parents, but again knew that was none of her business.

The evening had started badly and gone downhill from there, and at nine o'clock, using the excuse of school again, Phil took his leave without so much as a backward glance, as Flora waved awkwardly from the doorstep.

She hadn't even had a chance to talk to him about the threatening note she'd found. There just hadn't seemed to be the right time. Flora was having doubts now about showing it to P.C. Hughes anyway. From all accounts the man could barely manage finding the occasional lost cat. Surely, he couldn't be trusted with something as potentially serious as this. *No*, Flora

thought, *I'll take it into Morpeth myself later this week.*
Perhaps it was better if she kept the information secret
from everyone in the village.

As she tidied the kitchen, with Reggie perched on top
of one of the chairs at the small two-seater table,
something niggled at the back of Flora's mind. Her
main train of thought was directed at the disastrous
evening. She wasn't sure what had caused the change
in Phil – whether he had been in that mood when he'd
arrived, or actually become angry at something while
he was here – but he certainly wasn't the same man
she'd shared drinks with in the pub earlier in the week.
It was such a shame. She wasn't looking for a
relationship, her ex-husband had put her off that for a
long while to come, but a little companionship would
be nice. Flora hated her constant loneliness. Yet, all the
while these notions tumbled around in her tired head,
Flora had the rather annoying feeling that she was
missing something. Something terribly important at
that.

It wasn't until she was drying her face in the bathroom,
her pyjamas already on, and she called 'Peanut' for the
bird to settle down in the bedroom as was their new
nightly ritual, that it struck Flora. She had of course

used the name out of habit, but it brought her niggling problem to the front of her mind – if the parrot's real name was Reggie, why was he fixated on peanuts? He didn't even like eating them, as far as she was aware! When she had first arrived, in an effort to calm the bird down, Flora had bought him some peanuts – as recommended by a website dedicated to parrot care – and he couldn't have been less interested. No, the parrot must have a different reason for wanting to bring attention to the word. What it could be, however, Flora had no idea.

That was, until she had finished a chapter of her latest read – a bestselling, new release romance this time, as Flora was trying to get tips for her own book, if she ever managed to take the typewriter out of the box – and was snuggling down to sleep. Visions of the big house came to mind, the amount of work still to do with the paperwork, before anything could be started with regards to renovating the place. And how would she afford the renovations anyway? Perhaps some of the furniture could be rescued, reupholstered or made good and then reused? Certainly that coffee table in the front sitting room looked like antique walnut, that would polish up nicely…The table!.. The crumb!

The only other thing that had really caught Reggie's attention, apart from the word 'peanut', was the silly crumb which he wouldn't take his eyes off when they were at the house. Always cradling it in his talons. Could that be part of the puzzle? But it hadn't been on the table when he'd first found it, had it? It had been... under Harold's chair, close to where his body had been found! A shiver ran down Flora's spine and she pulled the blanket further up over her shoulders. As ridiculous as it seemed, she decided that she would collect that crumb, and any other in the vicinity of the armchair, and take them to the police station with the worrisome note. They would probably think her stupid, but at least Flora could rest easy knowing she had done all she could. Her father had been severely allergic to peanuts – it had been thought unusual by his doctors when he was a boy – though it was a lot more common nowadays. Perhaps, Flora thought as she yawned loudly, she'd try to find some medical papers in the piles of random mail, just in case Harold Baker had had a similar response to the nuts.

Feeling extremely unsettled, Flora fell into a fitful sleep, where ghosts of deceased relatives returned in the forms of birds – all sorts, from owls to chickens to parrots – and haunted her in her dreams.

SEVENTEEN

The next morning dawned cold and wet. Flora had a sinking feeling as she recalled that today was Thursday, and she was due to have dinner at the vicarage this evening. She tried to mentally shrug off the thought, though, as she had much to do between now and then. She had set her alarm and risen early, for she intended to make the short trip up to the manor house before opening the tearoom, both to collect the crumbs and to hunt around for any medical documents – past hospital discharge letters or the like, anything that would list Harold's known allergies. Dressing in some beige chinos and a light blue shirt adorned with tiny, embroidered daisies, Flora rushed a coffee and toast before wrapping a navy cardigan around her shoulders, throwing on her raincoat and heading out into what was now a downpour. "Lovely British summer," she muttered as she held her umbrella aloft and Reggie flew ahead, seemingly understanding her destination.

Thankfully, Flora had remembered to put some empty plastic sandwich bags in her handbag, and it was into one of these that she deposited the large crumb first. Reggie had perched himself on her back, keeping a close eye on proceedings. When he spied what she was doing, he joined Flora on the floor – she on her hands and knees and him stalking around her, squawking intermittently. Not for the first time, Flora wished she had had her eyes tested recently. Nevertheless, between them they found three more crumbs, though none as big as the first. It was when she was zipping up the bag, confident that she could see no more crumbs, that Flora realised Reggie had been talking to her. Certainly, the majority of the words had been his usual, 'peanut', but interspersed were 'good job', 'my Harold' and 'thank you kindly.' Flora was happier with this than she'd like to admit. It felt as if she had a partner, a companion at least, in all this, and she stroked the top of the bird's head appreciatively.

Her happiness was short lived, however, as Flora felt a sudden, sharp pain in her knee. Looking down, she saw a piece of broken china crockery, with a sharp edge poking through her trousers. Flora plucked it out, irritated, and put it into the bag with the crumbs, searching the floor and finding two more pieces to add to the collection. She wasn't sure what these meant, or if they were important, but it couldn't hurt to hand them to the police with her other findings.

Next they moved to the study. Unfortunately, the sudden deluge had meant that there was quite a soggy puddle on the rug, in the spot where the bucket had been previously, and Flora could have kicked herself for not returning it to its original place. That paled in comparison, however, when she looked up and saw the brown, damp mark on the ceiling, now positively ballooning with the water it carried. This side of the house was an extension to the original building, therefore all the room had sitting above it was a small attic space. Worried that the ceiling might collapse on her at any moment, Flora reluctantly decided to continue her search through the paperwork in the sitting room, although all she had found in there up to this point were brochures, adverts and reading material. Before returning to that room, however, she knew that she must try to at least catch the water which was dripping heavily from the bulge in the ceiling.

It was when Flora was trying to reach across a pile of papers to position the bucket successfully, that she slipped on the drenched floor and launched forwards, only breaking her fall by grabbing hold of an ornate candlestick on top of the elaborate wooden mantle. To her surprise, the wooden candle holder was fixed to the mantlepiece, as if it were part of that large installation. As such, it did not immediately budge even under the sudden influx of Flora's weight. After a couple of seconds, however, a squeaking and grinding sound filled the room as the candlestick moved haltingly to the left. *That accounted for the squeak, but what on earth was the grinding noise?* Flora wondered.

"Secrets and lies, secrets and lies," Reggie shrieked, as Flora's head whipped around to the right. There, beyond the mantlepiece, the rows of library shelves were shifting sideways, as a secret door was exposed. The grinding noise emanated from it sliding slowly to the right, just enough for a person to enter the unknown space beyond.

Flora was thrilled and terrified in equal measure. She relaxed her iron grip on the candlestick, realising that her knuckles were white and her back ached from the strange lunging position she was in. Righting herself, Flora looked around for Reggie, needing the comfort and reassurance of someone, anyone, even a feathered friend. Sensing her distress, he came and landed on her shoulder, saying "Ooh a secret! Ooh a secret!" as if repeating what he had heard many times in the past. Emboldened, Flora moved through the open hole in the wall. The smell of stale cigar smoke, of sweat and old papers assailed her, and at first she had to cover her nose. It was a small room, containing a mahogany desk with a green leather surface, a chair to match, and several filing cabinets. Unlike the other rooms she had seen, however, this space was completely organised. Shelves filled with labelled box files, everything orderly on the desk right down to the matching green fountain pen. Grabbing the chair, which was even heavier than it looked, Flora used it to wedge the doorway open – *just in case*, she told herself.

Reggie swooped to a small perch in the corner of the room – clearly put there for his use – and seemed perfectly comfortable in the space as if coming here was a common occurrence.

"Who's been naughty? Who's been naughty?" he chanted on repeat, making Flora unsure as to what he meant. That was, until she looked along the first shelf filled with box files. Each file had the name of a resident of the village – some Flora recognised and many she did not. Picking up the file titled 'Alf Drayford', whom she assumed to be Phil's father, Flora was shocked to see reams of handwritten pages detailing the man's accounts, both regarding rent to the estate and other items – things Harold Baker would have had no business knowing. There were photographs too, as if taken by a professional investigator, of the man kissing a woman – *not his wife?* Flora didn't want to speculate. Slamming the box closed, she found others, much fuller, some of which had their contents spread across two files, all incriminating whether financially or personally.

Disgusted, and needing some air, Flora decided to come back later to this room. Especially since there was another whole shelf of files which seemed to be labelled with different ventures: Whole Village Theme Park; Baker's Rise Bird Sanctuary; Manmade Fishing Lake; there were about thirty of them, with similar wacky, hairbrained schemes – it was clear now where all of Harold's money had gone and why there was nothing that remained to show for it.

For now, though, Flora needed a strong coffee and a trip to the police station in Morpeth with the note and the crumbs. Before leaving the space, however, she couldn't resist the urge to pull open the top drawer of the filing cabinet. Inside were matching blue cardboard manila files, each one carefully labelled. Maintenance Contracts, Manor Building works, Monthly Rents

Due… and so on, until Flora's eyes alighted on one that said Medical Bills. A brief look inside showed her that Harold had always chosen to go privately for his medical and dental work. Flora decided to take this with her, to look through at home, to check for allergies. She was about to slam the drawer closed when something caught her eye. It seemed out of place amongst the blue files – a clear, ziplocked folder. On instinct, Flora pulled that out too, shocked to see it contained pages of newspaper cuttings, some with specific letters snipped out from their headlines. A sick feeling settled in Flora's stomach. She had found her culprit. Harold had not been threatened, not by this method at least, rather he had been the one doing the deed. *Was he a blackmailer?* The evidence in the room would suggest so.

Flora fled the secret chamber with Reggie hot on her heels. She shoved the chair out of the way as she rushed past, then grabbed the candlestick and yanked it hard to the right, back to its original position. The loud grinding noise filled the room again as the secret door slid shut and the shelves hiding it moved back to their original position. Flora slowly released the breath she was holding. Things had just become much more sordid and she knew she had no choice now but to go to the police with what she had found.

EIGHTEEN

A shaken and wet Flora arrived some fifteen minutes later at the tearoom. It was only eight o'clock in the morning, yet she felt she had had enough of today's revelations already. She had decided to put up a small note in the café window, just in case any random ramblers or tourists should come across the place before she was able to open again that afternoon. George Jones was just pulling up in his baker's van as Flora unlocked the door to the tearoom, looking for her notebook and pen in her apron which was hung by the door.

"Morning Flora," he said cheerily, "sorry I'm a bit late, problem with the ovens."

"Don't worry," Flora said distractedly, "I think it's the morning for unexpected happenings."

George raised an eyebrow, especially when Reggie swooped down to land on his van roof, but said nothing else as he unloaded the day's supplies.

"Thank you," Flora took the box from him and shoved it on the nearest table, almost breaking a teacup as she did so.

"All alright? You look like you've seen a ghost!" George shuffled from one foot to the other awkwardly.

"Yes, just, ah, not opening up right away. Appointment... ah, ladies' issues!" *What on earth?* Of all the things she could have said, Flora was mortified that that was what her brain had directed her mouth to say. Her eyesight may be declining, her hair thinning and greying, and her curves slightly more padded, but she certainly hadn't hit the menopause yet! Besides, what was she doing sharing it with a man she barely knew? *Argh!* Flora screamed at herself inwardly.

"Oh! Right! I'll be off!" and George scarpered back to his van as if all the she-wolves of hell were on his tail!

Flora locked up, and grabbed the files she had hidden behind a plant pot, dismayed to hear another van coming up the short driveway. Of course, it would be Joe Stanton. She wouldn't be allowed to get away with not seeing him, today of all days!

"Morning Flossie," he began, though his usual merriment at her discomfort was cut short, when Reggie landed on Flora's shoulder and shouted, "Flora! Flora!"

It was the first time she had heard him say her name, and Flora could not have been happier that he had chosen now to do so. Joe looked suddenly unsure of himself, as Reggie launched himself from Flora's shoulder and aimed straight for the hapless postman, flapping his wings around the man's head, so that all Joe could do was to protect his face with the letters he was holding.

"Come here, Reggie," Flora said through a giggle she couldn't contain. There was certainly joy to be found in seeing this insufferable man get his comeuppance! Freed from the storm of feathers, Joe rushed forwards, slapped the letters into Flora's waiting hands and made a run for it back to his van, with Reggie chasing him the whole way.

"Good bird, good Reggie," Flora exclaimed happily, collecting her files and post and making her way hurriedly back to the coach house.

After giving Reggie a treat of some chopped apple and

banana, Flora gathered up the zip lock file of
incriminating cuttings, adding to it the sheet from the
typewriter box. She looked lovingly at the machine,
whispering, "I'll get you out as soon as I get back!"
Then she took a quick seat at the kitchen table and
flicked through the contents of the medical file... bills
for false teeth, verruca treatment, a mole biopsy... and
there, almost at the bottom of the pile, a discharge
letter from Wansbeck Hospital following removal of
the man's appendix. At the top of the letter, under the
dates and details of treatment administered, a list of
known allergies...only two were shown: Erythromycin
and Peanuts. Flora's feeling of dread returned, as the
implication of this began to sink in. The man was only
in his seventies when he died, and not in bad health
other than being overweight and having a penchant for
expensive cigars. He had angered a whole village, not
only by playing the 'lord of the manor' card regularly
with rent increases but apparently also by blackmailing
his neighbours. The only witness to his death, a parrot,
was fixated on peanuts, to which the man had been
severely allergic.

Harold's death certificate had shown the cause of
death as 'choking' but Flora began to suspect
something different. Something altogether more
sinister.

NINETEEN

The police station in Morpeth looked to have been designed and built in the 1970s – not the most attractive period in British architecture by a long way. Flora grabbed her plastic bag full of all the 'evidence' she had collected and made her way inside, feeling unsure of herself now that she was actually here. What on earth would they think of a middle-aged woman turning up to talk about a death from almost a year ago, of a man who seemingly died from a tragic accident? She was almost about to turn around and leave, calling herself a fool for her fanciful thoughts, when a good-looking man who had arrived behind her leaned forwards and held the door open. He was wearing a once-smart suit which was now a bit shiny around the edges, but his floppy brown hair and boyish grin caused butterflies to take flight in Flora's stomach.

"After you," he nodded his head in her direction, and Flora silently cursed her wayward hormones for the blush which spread across her cheeks. She rushed forwards, and in doing so tripped on a tiny step, causing her to lunge headlong, in a decidedly ungraceful manner. A strong arm reached out and grabbed her elbow, steadying her, and Flora looked up gratefully into a pair of twinkling brown eyes.

Thoroughly embarrassed now, Flora mumbled her thanks before joining the lengthy queue at the main desk. She couldn't help but sneak a glance from the corner of her eye, however, as the lovely man disappeared through one of the key-coded doors to the right.

After a wait of some forty minutes, during which time Flora almost gave up three times, she eventually reached the front desk. A rotund, balding man with huge round spectacles and an air of defeat looked at her expectantly, though spoke no question as to what he could help Flora with. Unsettled even further by his silence, Flora began blurting out the whole story, though in no particular order. Until, after a few minutes, red-faced and out of breath, she finally paused. The man had said nothing, made no expression other than boredom and had actually disappeared below the desk for a small part of the tale, apparently to find a mint.

Considering the effort hopeless, Flora was about to turn and leave when the sound of someone clearing their throat from the doorway to the glass-windowed office behind the desk caught her attention. On turning and seeing the owner of the noise, who just happened to be the man from the door incident, the desk policeman assumed a sudden air of efficiency and urgency. He produced an electronic tablet and began asking Flora in earnest her personal details and all the facts of her enquiry. The man behind them simply stood and listened in silence until, when Flora finished telling the story for the second time, he disappeared, re-emerging a moment later at the door to the side into which he had disappeared earlier. He invited Flora to come with him, and shortly after she found herself in an interview room.

It was the usual bare-walled, single-tabled situation – not that Flora would really know, since she had never been inside one in real life, her only point of reference being the detective shows she used to love to watch on TV when her ex-husband was 'working late.' Introducing himself as Detective Inspector Adam Bramble, and offering her a seat at the table, the man sat down opposite Flora, his long legs stretched out casually alongside them.

"So, Mrs. ah...," he paused to check the handheld computer he produced from his pocket, "Mrs. Miller. So, you now reside on the Baker Estate in Baker's Rise?"

"Yes," Flora suddenly felt as if she were under interrogation, though his pleasant demeanour had not changed, and the man looked at her from below his floppy fringe which gave him the air of a truanting schoolboy.

"Excellent. And how did you come by the lodging, and the... tearoom was it?.. after the death of the previous owner?"

Flora saw no point in lying, nor did she have a desire to. Keeping the truth from the villagers out of a misguided wish to fit in was one thing – and look how far that had got her – but lying, even by omission, to the police was a different matter entirely.

"I inherited the estate," she said, trying to keep her speech void of emotion, "out of the blue. Harold was my father's cousin once removed or some such relation, though my father never once mentioned him to me."

"And your father did not inherit because...?"

"He passed away eight years ago in a car accident, and my mother four years later from a stroke."

"I'm very sorry. So, you were the only living relative?"

"Apparently so. Harry Bentley, the solicitor – well he is formally retired, but continued looking after estate affairs at Mr. Baker's request – contacted me two months after the death. I have inherited it all, though it is starting to seem more and more like a poisoned chalice."

"Oh?" The detective's sudden eagerness made Flora realise she had chosen entirely the wrong word to describe her inheritance.

"What I mean," she rushed to add, "is that the main house is in dire need of repairs, I am suspicious about my benefactor's death, and the villagers are... insular to say the least."

"I see. So, you came to live in the big house?"

"No, I was going through a divorce and keen to move to the country, but I had the coach house and tearoom renovated with my own money. Aside from the assets – that is, the buildings, land and properties in the village – there was no cash to speak of. I suppose when the rents come in, I will be able to use them to start renovations, but I haven't thought that far ahead."

"Did you re-purpose those two buildings from scratch?"

"The coach house had been made fit for dwelling decades ago, so I had that done almost from scratch, new wiring, heating, the lot. The tearoom had been used as such up until four or so years ago, so that was more of a quick modernisation. I wanted the vintage look anyway."

"Okay. So, I will have to look up the death certificate for Mr. Baker, but you believe it attributes his cause of death to choking?"

"Yes, on food."

"I see. So, you have come to the village and are the new Lady of the Manor?"

"Yes, however the villagers think I am simply an employee of the new owner. Also, that I have been given custody of the man's parrot with the role."

"I was going to enquire as to why the subterfuge but... parrot? I have to say Mrs. Miller, your story is becoming more bizarre."

"I know. I can imagine how it must sound. The bottom line is, I wanted to fit in with my new neighbours so kept things close to my chest, and I've since discovered that the man I inherited it all from was a potential blackmailer, who frittered his money away on wild schemes and angered everyone whose landlord he was. I think that about sums it up. Oh, and I think one of those people hated him enough to kill him!" Flora paused, raising her hands in a signal of defeat.

"Very well. Despite the rather… unusual nature of your allegations, they are serious enough to warrant further investigation. Leave your, ah, cake crumbs and broken bits of crockery with me and I will have them tested in the lab. Give me all the evidence of a peanut allergy and the newspaper clippings and I will have those dusted."

"Thank you, Detective, though I do think they look rather more like scone crumbs than sponge – I've paid rather a lot of attention to the consistency of scones recently!" Flora got up to leave.

"Oh, and Mrs, Miller?"

"Yes?"

"Please try to stay out of bother until I get back in touch?"

"I'll try!" Flora blushed again as he led her from the room and back out into the drizzle. She took one look behind her as Detective Bramble retreated back into the building, before rushing to the sanctuary of her car.

TWENTY

The rest of the day passed thankfully without incident, as Flora had only one solitary customer in the tearoom, and rushed home at half past four to shower and change for her evening meal with the vicar and his wife. She had been considering cancelling all afternoon, but decided in the end that it was best just to get it over with. As she traipsed up the small path to the coach house, Flora was surprised to see a familiar figure waiting at her front door.

"Phil! This is a surprise!"

The man looked sheepish and uncomfortable. His left arm jutted out as Flora approached, "These are for you, to say sorry for being such a miserable oaf last night!"

Flora took the rather sad looking bunch of half-wilted

carnations, trying to look as grateful as possible despite her sore feet and tired heart.

"Yep, sorry about the state of them," Phil rushed on to fill the awkward silence, "they were the best Baker's Rise Essential Supplies had to offer!"

Flora made a mental note to never buy flowers from the local grocery store, and responded to Reggie's incessant flapping around Phil by unlocking the front door and letting the bird fly inside.

They hovered then on the doorstep, Flora aware that the clock was ticking down to her meal with the vicar.

"Look, I'm actual…"

"Sorry, you're clear…"

They laughed uncomfortably as both began speaking as once.

"Sorry," Phil said, "you're clearly busy. Can I take you for a drink in the pub later?"

"I'm actually going to the vicarage for tea."

"Really? Good luck with that one, rather you than me! Reverend Wright often comes to do assemblies at school and he could bore the hind legs off a donkey!"

"Oh no, really? Well perhaps I could text you afterwards? I'm planning to make my escape as soon as is polite! Then we could maybe meet at The Bun in the Oven if it's not too late?"

"Sounds perfect. Sorry again," and Phil walked off back down the driveway, raising his arm in a sad goodbye.

Flora rushed inside and slammed the door shut behind her with her foot. Reggie was hopping agitatedly from one foot to the other on the kitchen table.

"Stupid git!" he shouted in the direction of the front door.

"Reggie! That's rude! Who taught you that? Don't tell me... Harold. What do you have against Phil anyway?" Flora was troubled by the man. He was certainly attractive, but the parrot clearly didn't like him, Phil himself kept running hot and cold, and she didn't have the headspace right now to unravel it all. She put the limp floral offering into one of the cut crystal vases she had brought from her home in London and rushed to get washed and changed for the daunting meal ahead.

Flora pushed open the small garden gate at the bottom of the path which led up to the vicarage, feeling not a small amount of trepidation. The grass on either side was well tended, and small flowers adorned the edges of the worn paving slabs. The vicarage itself sat to the side of the church on the village Green, though slightly elevated, giving it a view across the Green, duck pond, Front street, and of the road which ran straight through Baker's Rise.

Flora had decided that this was one of those occasions that required the 'power dressing' from her life of old, and so had opted for a tailored linen suit in pale blue, a delicate cream blouse with lace collar, and high, strappy sandals. She looked the part, even if she didn't feel it. The vicarage door opened before Flora had reached the top of the path and she was met with a small, stern-looking, spectacled woman, dressed in a thick tweed skirt, grey shirt buttoned to her chin, and thick knitted cardigan, which belied the warmth of the summer evening. She did not smile nor even acknowledge Flora's presence, other than to stand to the side of the doorway to allow the other woman to enter.

"I am Enid Wright, wife to the vicar of this parish," she said formally as she closed the large door and directed Flora into a room to the side with a tiny, bony hand.

"Pleased to meet you, I am Flora Miller, though I suspect you know that." Flora sat on the high-backed, wing chair as directed, placing her clutch bag delicately on the coffee table beside her. Enid looked Flora up and down, not bothering to disguise her perusal, and Flora felt like an animal on display in a zoo. Eventually, Enid herself sat down, on the other side of the roaring fire. Flora could already feel herself beginning to sweat – why on earth they would have a full log fire going in the middle of summer she had no idea. She desperately wanted to stand up and remove her thin suit jacket, but her fear of once again being under Enid's scrutiny was greater than Flora's current discomfort.

"So," the vicar's wife said eventually, "you have come to live on the Baker Estate." It was a statement rather than a question, yet Flora felt compelled to answer.

"Yes, I live in what was the coach house and run the tearoom."

"Indeed, that tearoom used to do great business when someone local was in charge – did you know that I used to work there occasionally?"

"No, no I did not," if the woman was fishing for a job, then this lake was certainly empty! "Is your husband not joining us?"

"For the meal, yes, he is an extremely busy man as you can imagine."

Flora couldn't really imagine how a rural vicar with less than a few hundred parishioners could be that occupied, but nodded her head anyway. "How long has he been the parish incumbent?" she asked, trying to turn conversation away from her role on the estate.

"Eight years come December. So, are you the new lady of the manor then?" the words were almost spat across the space between them, nothing wasted on civility nor any attempt to wrap the question in flowery language.

Flora shifted uncomfortably on the hard chair and decided it was pointless trying to hide the fact any longer – they all disliked her anyway, "Yes, well I wouldn't give myself that title, but I have inherited the estate, yes."

Enid clicked her tongue against her teeth, sucked in her breath noisily and finally spoke, "Well, I do say. My husband will need to hear of this."

"I don't really see any rea..." Flora began but was rudely interrupted.

"So, let us leave talk of that until later. For now, I wish to discuss the village fete."

"The fete?" Flora was positively boiling now, and stood up abruptly to remove her jacket. How the other woman could bear sitting in this sweltering room wearing a thick cardigan, Flora didn't know. Perhaps she felt the cold more at her age, which Flora estimated at around the mid fifties, though she had the dress sense and air of a woman closer to Betty Lafferty's age.

"Yes, the fete. Now, you may know that I am the master baker in the village, winning the Scone Competition and the Victoria Sponge Contest every year since arriving here."

"Though you are not the current holder of the title, are you?" Flora couldn't help but poke the hornet's nest now, she had had enough of being the underdog in this conversation, "I'm sure Betty Lafferty told me that she won last year?"

"Well!" Enid turned red then white, then stood and rushed over to an old-fashioned writing escritoire in the corner. She lifted the wooden lid, fished in the drawers and produced several brightly coloured ribbons, "Here!" she shoved them towards Flora who, on closer inspection saw that they were rosettes. They had clearly once been on display, as they still had the fixings – though these looked to have been ripped away from the wall at some point - and all were slightly faded from the sun. Perhaps Enid had taken them down in anger when she lost the title? It was clearly an extremely sensitive subject.

"Very nice," Flora gave them a cursory look and put the awards down beside her handbag.

"I hear you have been taking lessons from the farmer's wife?" Enid, now composed again, spoke the title as if it were a derogatory term.

Flora could not see how she'd found out, nor what business it was of hers, but nevertheless she nodded in reply.

"Well, you would do well to learn from the best. I can offer you my teaching for a nominal donation towards the church roof fund."

Flora coughed to hide her shock and amusement. As if she would pay this woman for anything! "Thank you, I am very happy with Lily's instruction. Indeed, after just one lesson I am making great progress."

Enid make a noise akin to a snort of disbelief, but they were thankfully interrupted at that very moment by the man himself, Reverend Wright. "Cook has just left. The pie is ready to be served," he muttered from the doorway, with not a word of greeting to Flora.

What a rude couple, she thought to herself, making a silent promise to not give them an inch when it came to requests for either her funds or her time.

TWENTY-ONE

The dining room was a dismal creation of dark wood
and deep maroon velvet which had seen many better
days, in the distant past no doubt. Flora sat where she
was directed once again, regretting leaving her bag and
coat in the other room. She would eat as quickly as
possible and then make her escape to the pub with
Phil. Anything was better than this interrogation. They
were halfway through the meal, and already the vicar
had quizzed her on the two times she had been seen
driving out of the village – his study must face the road
and he clearly had too much time on his hands, as well
as being an insufferable busybody just like his wife.
Talk then turned to the tearoom, and whether Flora
would be donating half of the profits to the church
fund as her predecessor had. Apart from the fact she
had not yet looked for any proof at the manor house to

substantiate the claim, and felt a deep mistrust for this man despite his ecumenical status, Flora would not have said yes in a thousand years anyway. It was not their business that she was yet to make anything but a loss on the venture. Yet the pushy couple proceeded to coerce and cajole, seemingly thick-skinned to any rebuttal.

Flora batted away their requests increasingly firmly, until finally she laid her knife and fork down on her plate, wiped her mouth on the rather grubby linen napkin, and stood abruptly from her chair.

"Vicar, Mrs Wright, thank you for the meal. I can confirm with absolute certainty that I will not be donating to your roof fund, either from the estate or from my own income from the tearoom. I will not be requiring any teaching in the baking department either!" She added, just to sever all ties, before stalking from the room, collecting her belongings, and letting herself out. The sight of their open-mouthed faces, totally shocked at being spoken to like that, brought a schoolgirlish giggle up from Flora's chest as soon as she was out in the refreshingly fresh air.

She felt a rush of adrenaline, such as she had felt the day she left her husband. It had taken her years to get to the point where she would stand up to him, and she had promised herself from that point onwards to always be more assertive in the future. Well, she had kept that promise, and it felt glorious! Flora practically skipped down the path. She knew there would be consequences, of course, from upsetting the couple, but right now Flora cared not a jot! She quickly texted Phil that she would meet him at the end of his street, as he lived in Cook's Row just behind the Green, and then wandered that way still high on her victory.

The street sign brought another chuckle to Flora's throat, though she did have to do a double-take to check she was in the right place. The second 'o' in cook had been half painted out so it now looked like a 'c'.

"How do you feel about living on 'Cock's Row'?" Flora asked, giggling, as Phil appeared out of the second house on the left.

Her amusement and bubbly mood was seemingly infectious, as Phil chuckled along with her.

"Well, it's better than last year when they changed the second word to 'Rise' to go with it!" he laughed, linking Flora's arm through his. They sauntered slowly down to the pub, as Flora described her time at the vicarage and the impromptu ending it had suffered. Phil couldn't believe it and congratulated Flora heartily for standing up to the nauseating pair.

"They have ruled the roost for far too long in this village," he said, "now Harold is gone, it's time for them to move on too! Let me buy you a drink to celebrate."

Flora accepted his offer gratefully, and the pair found a table at the front of the pub, near to the door, where they settled themselves with a pint of Guinness and a glass of red wine. Phil once again apologised for his previous foul mood, citing new worries over the possible closure of the village school as the cause. He went on to say, however, that he had had a brainwave that very morning, and planned to make a stall at the summer fete, with old photos of classes from yesteryear. He hoped the villagers would enjoy reminiscing and might order copies of the black and white mementos, for a small contribution to school funds. If the local newspaper could be persuaded to take some photos and write an article on how the school was an integral part of village life, then the council might sit up and take notice. Flora thought this a great idea and offered to help Phil sort through the photos and try to identify year groups and people still living locally, though her knowledge on this was still very limited. It seemed like a fun project, though, and a way to learn a bit more about her neighbours.

In talking about this plan, Flora herself came up with a

great idea – why wait until the fete, which was still over a month away, to begin the project? What if she displayed some of the old photos in the tearoom as well? It would be a reason for the locals to come and visit the place, to have a look and see who they recognised. Then, maybe in a week or two, Flora could hold an event at the café, maybe an afternoon tea, to attract them all together. It would kill two birds with one stone for her and Phil alike. Like a mini fundraiser of sorts.

Phil heartily agreed with the plan and said he would bring a pile of photos from the old storeroom at the school around next Monday evening, as he was going away with his rambling group at the weekend. They were just finishing their drinks, when Doctor Edwards arrived with his wife. Immaculately dressed again, in fact looking film star-glamorous compared to the dowdy couple with whom she had just shared a meal, Edwina Edwards paused by Flora and Phil's table as she passed.

"I'm not sure we have been introduced," she said with a haughty air and a cut-glass accent, "I am Mrs. Edwards. My husband is the local physician."

Flora wondered why all of the women she'd met today referred to themselves only in the light of their husband's occupation. Something niggled in the back of Flora's mind, but she didn't have the time or the mental capacity right now to focus on it. Instead she simply stood, her back straight and her air one of independence and authority. Emboldened by her earlier steadfastness, and seeing no reason to continue keeping secrets, Flora refused to cow tow to these people any longer.

"Flora Miller. I am the new owner of The Rise," she said, hearing Phil's surprised intake of breath from behind her and enjoying the look of shock on Edwina Edwards' face. The whole public house seemed to fall silent, and all eyes were on Flora. She would not back down now, though. Instead she turned to face the whole room and said, "Yes, you heard me correctly, I am Flora Miller. Proprietor of your new café, the Tearoom on The Rise, and also the new owner of Baker's Rise."

The hushed silence was broken only by Ray coughing and spluttering behind the bar, and Doctor Edwards walking back to re-join his wife.

In a somewhat stilted voice, the doctor said, "Welcome to the village, Mrs. Miller, I'm sure my neighbours will all join me in extending our friendship and hospitality." There was a murmur from the small group assembled, though other than Joe Stanton, Flora saw no one else that she recognised among them.

"I knew it!" The postman said, in a very self-congratulatory manner. Flora fixed her shrewd eyes on him and he quickly sat back down in his seat. How he had suspected the fact, she would discuss with him the next time he delivered the post. The new, confident Flora would no longer allow him to embarrass and belittle her. If he was illegally opening people's mail then she would find out. Just as she would find out exactly what had happened to poor Harold.

TWENTY-TWO

The next morning dawned bright and fair, and Flora was determined to seize the day with both hands. Thankful that she and Phil had parted ways after just the one drink, so she had no headache to deal with, Flora was at the tearoom before George Jones arrived with the day's baked goods. She was hoping to catch Joe Stanton and have a word with him about her suspicions regarding his postal tampering, but was not at all surprised when she found the few letters simply sitting on her doorstep when she opened the door to a delivery driver later that morning. It was Reggie's new daytime perch for the tearoom, ordered online the previous day. The village postman was clearly avoiding her, but Flora knew that in a community as small as Baker's Rise he couldn't hide for long!

Flora was determined that even the lack of customers would not bother her this day, as she pottered around cleaning the chinaware and mopping the floors. She had just sat down for a well-earned break, with Reggie beside her enjoying a treat of two large, green grapes. Flora herself was enjoying a cream éclair – it needed eating as it went out of date that day, so Flora justified it to herself that way. She wanted to look trim for the big afternoon tea event. Flora had her laptop in front of her and was designing the flyers now. She considered printing them herself, but then decided to go all out and get a shop in Morpeth to do it for her. It was her big launch, as well as the school support event, so she decided to make the effort to have as much as possible done professionally. Besides, there was not much time to organise everything.

The flyers were almost finished and ready to be emailed across when the bell above the door tinkled.

"Somebody else! Somebody else!" Reggie shouted excitedly, immediately discarding what was left of his second grape and flying up to greet the customer.

"Reggie! Stop! You'll frighten them off!" Flora raised her voice as she stood and turned to welcome her guest. Standing there was none other than Pat Hughes' wife.

"Good morning, I am Tanya Hughes, my husband is the village policeman," she said in excellent English, holding out a very well-manicured hand.

Again with the male attachment, Flora thought, but fixed a smile on her face and held out her hand in return, "Flora Miller, it's lovely to meet you."

The two women shook hands, whilst Tanya used her other hand to flap at Reggie, who was swooping at her head from different angles.

"She's a corker! She's a corker!" he shouted animatedly. Tanya didn't seem too fazed by him though. She simply stared the bird straight in the eye and said firmly, "Desist you stupid creature!" To Flora's surprise, Reggie took the words to heart and flew straight back to his new perch.

"I'll have to try that with him next time," Flora laughed as she offered Tanya a seat at a table next to the far window, with views of the lawns and trees beyond, "I'm afraid he's picked up some rather questionable phrases from his previous owner!"

Tanya laughed with her and sent the bird another warning look.

"Here's the menu," Flora indicated the beautifully

typed and laminated sheet on top of the table, decorated with paintings of flowers and bunting.

"Thank you, Flora, I will take a pot of fruit tea, please, though I actually came to speak to you."

Not someone else begging for money, Flora thought, though she simply moved to behind the counter and put on the kettle, "I have Elderflower, Chamomile, Mixed Berries or Mango and Passion fruit."

"Mixed berries would be perfect, thank you," Tanya stood to stand on the opposite side of the counter. She reached out a hand and stroked the large coffee monster, "Beautiful machine you have here. I used to live in London and worked as a barista until I met my former partner. He was a strict Russian and did not like the idea of me working."

Flora's ears perked up, she had so many questions! "I lived in London too, I'm just recently divorced," she had no idea why she led with that, but Flora felt immediately at ease with Tanya, just as she had with Lily Houghton and Betty Lafferty "are you yourself from Russia?"

"Close. I am from Ukraine. I am glad to not live in London any longer. I was not so happy there as I am here."

"Indeed, me neither," Flora smiled, "so, you could work this machine? Do you think you could teach me?"

"Of course!" Tanya moved to the other side of the counter and turned on the coffee maker.

"Oh, your beautiful clothes!" Flora suddenly realised that Tanya was looking very smart in a fine-knit longline teal jumper and white leather leggings, "let me get you an apron. That monster tends to spurt steam and milk over every outfit!"

"Ah, thank you, but I am sure it will be fine, I love your shoes by the way, such a pretty shade of yellow," Tanya took the apron and tied it deftly, before turning her attention to the coffee machine.

"Thank you, they're from a small shop down one of the cobbled lanes in Sorrento, such beautiful leather they have there in Italy. I have the matching handbag somewhere too," Flora said wistfully, "to be honest, I have far too many shoes, handbags and clothes. You should come round sometime and see if there's anything you fancy!"

Tanya seemed extremely grateful for the offer, and within two minutes she had the machine purring like a kitten and was well on the way to making the perfect latte.

"Well I never!" Flora exclaimed happily, "Thank you so much, let's sit with the fruit tea, then if you wouldn't mind giving me a quick lesson..?"

"Not at all, I have something to ask of you as well," Tanya replied, resuming her seat.

Here we go, Flora thought, though she felt much more well-disposed to helping Tanya after the coffee maker revelation! "What can I help you with?"

"Well, you may have noticed, there are not so many ladies of our age or younger in the village," Tanya began, before rushing quickly on, "just us two, Shona who is Ray's daughter, Amy in the hairdresser's and a couple of others, and I am starting a venture – an exercise class – so I was hoping you might give it a try? In the church hall on Wednesday evenings from next week. I'm hoping that eventually some ladies from nearby villages will come too," she blushed furiously, as if she had asked for money.

To be honest, it had been so long since Flora had done much exercise of any sort that she would almost rather have been asked for a monetary contribution instead! Nevertheless, she sought further details from her new friend, "What kind of exercise is it?" Flora hoped it would be something calm like yoga or Pilates.

"It's called Baker's Rise Jazzercise – perfect for getting the heart pumping and a bit of a boogie too!"

"Well, I think you may have a rather misplaced confidence in my dancing skills," Flora laughed, though she took the offered flyer and read it through, before eventually saying, "Go on then, sign me up for four classes and we'll see how I get on!"

"Eek!" Tanya shrieked gleefully and came around the table to hug Flora. It was so long since anyone had hugged her, that Flora was embarrassed to feel tears spring to her eyes. She laughed to cover her feelings and stood with her teacup in hand, "in return , you can make me a barista extraordinaire!"

"Deal!" Tanya hugged Flora again, and their friendship was sealed.

They had practised making cappuccinos, lattes and a simply americano, until Flora felt that she would be able to remember how to do it when she no longer had Tanya by her elbow guiding her kindly. They chatted about life in London, the slower pace of things in the countryside, and then cake making. Tanya admitted that she had tried last year to enter a cake from her home country into the village fete's 'Free Style' baking competition, only to have it disqualified because it was not a traditional British recipe. She hinted that there had been a huge kerfuffle at the fayre last year, due to the Scone Competition not being won by the usual recipient. Flora put two and two together and knew she was talking about Enid Wright, but did not say as much. Apparently there had been accusations of cheating and favouritism, and Tanya had been relieved in the end not to be involved in such cake wars!

It was as the two women were talking of scones, and other such treats, that who other should arrive but Lily Houghton, as if she had been conjured by their conversation.

"Afternoon ladies," she greeted them cheerfully, her red cheeks and glowing smile always a welcome sight. Flora checked the clock and realised it was indeed afternoon – the time had flown now that she had someone to share it with.

"Afternoon, Lily," Flora said happily, "I was just going to make us some sandwiches. Would you care to join us?"

"Ooh that would be lovely," Lily exclaimed sitting down heavily on the nearest chair, "I'll just take the weight off my feet. I've been working in the farm shop all morning, but now the vet's up at the farm with my Stan as a sheep is having problems. Both the men in their element and the farm shop is closed Friday afternoons for me to catch up on housework, so I thought I'd treat myself to a walk into the village!" she breathed heavily and Reggie came to land beside Lily, rubbing his head into her arm.

"She's a keeper!" he chirped – it seemed everyone liked the lovely woman.

"Perfect, well you're very welcome," Flora said, as a thought suddenly struck her, "but perhaps you'd like to help me make a batch of fruit scones to go with our sandwiches?" she said it sheepishly, as Flora knew the request was a bit cheeky. So far this day she had had two customers and had roped them both into helping her!

"Of course, my dear, you only had to ask!" Lily jumped up again and began teaching Flora and Tanya how to make the simple scone recipe. Flora whipped out her notebook and took down the instructions once again, as she listened intently to each step. Half an hour later they were all sitting down together with a big pot of fruit tea for Tanya, a cappuccino for Flora and latte for Lily, scones hot from the oven and a plate of cheese and pickle sandwiches. Perfection.

The three women chatted as they ate, until reluctantly Lily said she had to get back to the farm. Flora had shared with them both the school photo idea and the afternoon tea event, and they had promised to come and help her on the day. They offered their services for free, but Flora knew she would pay her new friends for their help, she was so grateful.

Flora was finally beginning to feel more at home. She had friends and a pet, a lovely little home and a handsome man to have drinks with. All she needed was to sort the cloud of Harold and the manor house which was hanging over her, and then she could really begin to enjoy her new life.

TWENTY-THREE

Flora's bubble burst at four thirty that afternoon as she was locking up for the day and noticed an unfamiliar car pull up alongside her own. She was planning to just leave her car there for the night rather than driving it up to the garage at the manor house, as it was only two minutes' walk for her to the coach house anyway, and so she went across to greet the stranger and tell them she had just closed for the day. Reggie flew above her, squawking his impatience as he wanted to go home for his teatime meal. Distracted by the bird, it was not until he was fully out of the vehicle that Flora recognised the attractive features of Detective Bramble.

"Mrs. Miller," he said as the man straightened to his full height.

He must be at least six foot five, Flora thought to herself, but aloud she replied, "Detective Bramble. I would say this is a lovely surprise, but I fear your appearance here so soon after my visit to the station must mean that you have news for me?"

"Indeed. Let me introduce my colleague Detective Blackett," Bramble gestured back to the car, where a small, bird-like man with greased-back hair was hopping out of the passenger's side.

"Detective Blackett," Flora merely nodded her head to accompany the name and looked back to Bramble.

"Is there somewhere we can talk privately, Mrs. Miller?"

"Yes, my home is just up this path."

"Excellent. Lead the way. Or rather, let's follow that parrot!"

The trio made their way up to the coach house. The footpath was too narrow between the trees and bushes for them to walk in anything but single file, but after a moment they arrived at the old, wooden door of the coach house.

"Watch out! Watch out! Hide it all!" Reggie shouted, much to Flora's embarrassment as she fumbled in her bag for her keys. He made it sound like she was the one with something to hide.

Detective Bramble simply grinned at the bird and then at Flora, whilst his dour colleague showed no emotion whatsoever. Yet again, Flora was embarrassed by the state of her clothing, waiting to be unpacked and still piled up in the hallway and sitting room. She silently vowed, for the thousandth time, to sort it out at the weekend. The three navigated their way into the small lounge area, which seemed even tinier with the large presence of Adam Bramble filling half of the room. The two men perched on the settee, whilst Flora took the armchair beside the fire. They refused her offer of coffee politely, clearly keen to get to the business of their visit.

"Ooh, secrets and lies, secrets and lies," Reggie chirped happily, finding a perch on the arm of Flora's chair, despite her efforts to shoo him into his cage.

"Fine bird," Bramble commented, a twinkle in his eye, as he looked at Flora. For a moment, she had the notion that he was referring to her, but then shook her head to clear it of such frivolous ideas.

"Thank you, I inherited him with the estate, but he has become a good companion – of sorts!" Flora shrugged her shoulders and stroked Reggie's green feathers lightly. Blackett was obviously a man of even fewer words than he had expressions, and sat in stoic silence throughout.

"So, what have you to tell me?" Flora enquired, her curiosity piqued.

"Well, following your request that we analyse the papers and the crumbs, we believe there may be a case of foul play to investigate."

"Really?" Flora was shocked. She hadn't actually believed in her heart that Harold had been murdered, had she? It had all been fanciful speculation up until this point.

"The crumbs have tested positive for peanut. We cannot tell how big of a dose, given the small amount of the scone remnants you provided. However, given Mr. Baker's allergic status, which according to his records was a reaction of an immediate and anaphylactic nature, even a small amount would be enough to kill him if adrenaline was not immediately administered in the form of an Epi pen or suchlike. The newspaper clippings and cut-out letters have no fingerprints on them at all, suggesting the person who handled them was wearing gloves to avoid detection."

The room fell into silence as Flora absorbed this

information. After what felt like a long minute, she asked, "so, you will be beginning an investigation?"

"We will. Tomorrow morning in fact. I will have uniformed officers taking statements around the village, to narrow down a short list of suspects, who will then be interviewed by Detective Blackett and myself."

"I could help you!" Flora blurted out, though where the thought came from she had no idea, she had enough on her plate as it was. Mind you, she did feel she owed it to Harold – however tenuous the blood-link between them – to get to the truth of his death. She sank back into her chair, her cheeks blushing wildly as the embarrassment coursed through her.

"I could help you! I could help you!" Reggie repeated, refusing to let her offer die. For a brief moment, Flora felt like strangling the bird, until he was interrupted by one of their guests.

"Well, we don't normally encourage members of the public to interfere…" Blackett spoke for the first time. His voice was low and gruff, completely the opposite to the shrill, high sound Flora had attached to him in her mind given his smaller stature. He spoke sternly, and stared at Flora as he did so.

"On this occasion, though," Bramble jumped in quickly, flashing Flora with his handsome smile, "I think it might be beneficial, at least in the early stages, to have some local knowledge on hand. Thank you, Mrs. Miller, I shall call around for you at nine tomorrow morning if I may?"

"Of course!" Flora couldn't keep the shock from her voice or her face, and felt like giggling, totally inappropriately, as Reggie shouted, "There'll be hell to pay!" three times in quick succession.

TWENTY-FOUR

When the two detectives had left, and Reggie was
finally fed and calmed, Flora sat down with a glass of
red wine and a cheese and ham toastie. Her heart had
settled into more of a normal rhythm after the
revelations of earlier in the evening, and she could
think a bit more clearly about the whole situation. By
the time she'd finished off her light meal, Flora had
come to two decisions. First, that she could not discuss
this with Phil, as much as she wished to. Not even
Harry Bentley, she decided sadly. As no-one could be
ruled out at the moment, and all must come under
suspicion – herself included, she assumed.

The second decision had to do with the typewriter,
which up until now had remained in its box on the
kitchen table. Flora had told herself initially that this

was because it contained the delicate evidence of a threatening note, which had been handed to Detective Bramble yesterday with the rest of the papers. She hadn't wanted to add extra fingerprints to the sheet. After that, though, when Flora still couldn't bring herself to unbox the machine, she had to admit that it was because she felt a certain amount of trepidation – a fear of failure, to be honest. All her life she had wanted to write a novel, now she had the time and the means, and she was afraid she'd turn out to be... well, mediocre at best. So, decision number two was that the typewriter would come out of its box. Right now, this very evening, and Flora would use it to compile a list of the people in the village whom she knew to have had some connection to Harold Baker. A list she could certainly manage. Baby steps... maybe she would start the romance book this weekend.

Flora's hands shook as she lifted the heavy, gunmetal-grey typewriter out of the container. Whilst the machine itself looked pristine, the box itself had seen better days and smelt musty and off. Removing all the ink ribbons and instructions, Flora discarded the box outside her front door, ready to take to the recycling bin next to the tearoom the next morning. That task complete, she set the typewriter on the table and tried to work out how to thread the ribbon. Her grandfather had had a very similar model to this when she was a young girl, and Flora had loved hammering away on the keys to produce gobbledegook, but she had no idea for the life of her how to input the ink.

Some half an hour later, a much redder, decidedly more irritated Flora finally had victory over the machine! It had cost her a broken nail, and Reggie had learnt some new, rather colourful language, but it was done. A sheet of paper into the spool and she was ready to roll!

Flora did feel rather guilty that she was about to make notes on her neighbours, even the ones she had no reason to dislike, but it helped sort through her thoughts, so that she wouldn't end up tongue-tied in front of the lovely Detective Bramble the next morning.

At nine o'clock prompt on Saturday morning, the doorbell at the coach house rang indicating Detective Bramble's arrival. Flora was sweating and flustered, having just run back up from the tearoom in rather unsuitable heeled sandals. She had texted Tanya the previous evening, when inspiration struck, and asked her to man the fort for her at work this morning. Tanya was thrilled to be asked, and refused to take any payment for the favour, though Flora intended to pop some money in an envelope for her later. Having unlocked the tearoom and quickly shown Tanya the ropes, then raced to the manor house to open the side door for the forensics team, Flora was back just in time to open the door to the delectable detective. She let out a sigh of relief to see he was without his sombre partner today.

"Mrs Miller," Bramble tipped his head in acknowledgement and followed Flora into the kitchen, where her typed list remained in the typewriter.

"Good morning, Detective. I was busy yesterday evening, after you left, and have prepared some information that you may find useful during your investigations," Flora turned the roller knob on the side of the machine to release the paper and handed the black and white sheet to the man opposite. He smiled his thanks, and from this close distance Flora could see the small lines around his eyes. She couldn't tell whether they were from laughter or worry, but imagined it to be the former.

Bramble scanned the document quickly and pursed his lips.

"I hope it's okay," Flora was suddenly unsure of herself, "please do keep it confidential, I wouldn't want my neighbours to think I am always this...

scathing."

"Of course… may I call you Flora?"

"Certainly!" Flora felt herself blushing.

"Of course, Flora, this is excellent, really, very useful insights. Let me just clarify a few points with you before we set off," he smiled gently and Flora felt her cheeks flame a deeper red at his praise. Her ex-husband had not had a positive word to say about her for many years before they separated, and Flora reacted as if she were starved of the reassurance.

"Thank you," she whispered, her eyes tipped down towards the floor shyly, "fire away!"

"Excellent, shall we sit?"

"By all means," Flora led them both into the sitting room, where Reggie, who had been snoozing happily on his perch, suddenly came to life, fluffing his feathers and preening.

"Visitors!" he squawked happily, "Visitors with money!"

"No!" Flora was mortified, "Not money, you silly bird!" Bramble chuckled and reached out to tickle Reggie on his head feathers. Flora released the breath she had been holding. Was she to be embarrassed every day by her feathered companion? As Reggie was finding his voice again, so too his confidence was growing, and Flora was beginning to realise that he had a very cheeky side – with decidedly no filter!

"So," Bramble began as he sank down onto the sofa, stretching his long legs out in front of him, "tell me more about these rents."

"Well," Flora took her favourite chair beside the fire, suddenly aware she had been a terrible hostess and not offered the man a drink, but to do so now, when they had just begun talking business, seemed inappropriate. She made a mental note to take him into the tearoom later.

"Flora?"

"Sorry, Detective, yes, well as you know I am the new owner of The Rise and the estate which goes along with it. It would seem the estate thrived in the decades before Harold Baker inherited it and frittered away any income. The village was therefore built up around the manor house in times past, as workers on the estate needed cottages to live in, and amenities for provisions. For this reason, many of the buildings in the village belong to the Baker estate, and as such they pay rent monthly. Harry Bentley, retired solicitor of the community, still handles the estate's business affairs."

"And you trust him?"

"Completely, yes."

"But the residents disapprove of the rent increases which your predecessor imposed on them."

"Exactly," Flora sighed, "it is something I need to look into and discuss with Harry, the rents need to be lowered in line with market rates."

"So, many of his tenants would have had reason to be angry with Mr. Baker?"

"All of them, yes, especially Stan Houghton up at the farm, and Ray Dodds at the local pub, as their incomes may well have fluctuated downwards whilst the rents continued in an upward trajectory," Flora watched Bramble taking notes in a small black notepad as he listened to her responses.

"Very well. Now, you mention here the Vicar – a Reverend Francis Wright – is he a tenant too?"

"No, I believe the chapel and vicarage belong to the Church of England, so strictly speaking the vicar is their tenant and the home comes with his role as parish clergyman. He did have a strange relationship with

Harold though, I think. The tearoom that I now own and run was open up until a few years ago, and the vicar is adamant that half of the profits from the place were given by Harold to the church roof funds. I haven't had a chance to substantiate this claim yet, and it does seem strange, given what I know of Harold and his tight grasp on his purse strings where the village was concerned. He didn't even do the small repairs which his tenants requested, so I'm told. Anyway, the reverend was most put out when he lost this donation when the tearoom closed, and is still disgruntled about it now."

"I see," Bramble was scanning Flora's list again now, "and the doctor – I know from checking the death certificate yesterday that it was your local Dr. Edwards who examined the deceased and signed the death certificate."

"Really? So he was the one who decided it was choking?"

"Indeed. Did he have anything against Mr. Baker? Of course, he would know about the peanut allergy from having access to the man's medical records."

"Well, from that point of view, then so did his wife – she is the receptionist at his practice."

"Is she now? Very interesting," Bramble wrote this down, "and the anonymous threatening notes, do you know who could have received those?"

"Anyone and everyone, I suppose. Whilst I don't want to think of Harold as a blackmailer..." Flora's thoughts trailed off and she left the word hanging between them.

"Well, quite. So, obviously those who received those threats might suspect him as the sender, but would anyone else know? You mention here that the postman seems suspicious?"

"Yes, Joe Stanton, a rather dislikeable man, but apart from my personal feeling I would lay money on the fact that he is tampering with the mail."

"Okay, well, I think that gives us enough to go on for now. Perhaps you would join me for a walk around the village? Just to orient myself? And then a trip up to the manor house to look at the documents still there? Thank you for unlocking the door in readiness this morning, the tech team will be there dusting for prints and searching for more crumbs and shards of crockery now."

"Of course," Flora stood to put Reggie in his cage.

"Oh, and Flora?"

"Yes?"

"Why did you bring this matter straight to the main station in Morpeth and not to your local police constable?"

"You'll see when you meet him," Flora raised her eyebrows and Bramble gave her an enquiring smile in response. This would be an interesting morning indeed.

TWENTY-FIVE

The sun was shining through the clouds, though a strong northerly wind brought more than a little chill to the air. Flora wished she had brought at least a cardigan to warm her bare shoulders in her pretty sundress, but unfortunately she had been more focused on Detective Bramble's broad back as they left the house, than on her own comfort. Nevertheless, the morning had fared well so far. They had ambled around the small village, with Flora pointing out the school, church and the few other landmarks she recognised. Bramble had made notes of various locations in his pad and had nodded, though conversation was scarce when he was concentrating.

Then, at his request, Flora had introduced the detective to Ray Dodds in the pub, as the man was preparing to open for the day, and they were both given short shrift. Ray didn't seem so keen to flirt when he learned Flora was accompanied by a man of the law. He shifted furtively from one foot to the other as he polished a glass behind the bar, and refused to make eye contact with either of them. His greasy hair, normally slicked back, had tumbled forward and was obscuring half of his forehead, displaying a large bald patch on the top of his scalp. The thought of him as some sort of ladies' man, a local Lothario, no longer made Flora giggle as it had that night in the pub with Phil. Rather, she felt quite sick at the thought. The smell of stale body odours and beer assailed her, and Flora was glad when Bramble made their excuses to leave. Blinking as they walked out of the dingy building and back into the bright sunlight, Flora gulped in the fresh air greedily. Her nerves calmed a little, when Bramble made her smile with his quick wit.

"Hardly a ray of sunshine," he chuckled, "do you think his mother named him out of a sense of irony?"

Flora laughed with him, though a sense of unease was creeping over her at the seriousness of their mission. She could see a few uniformed officers moving door to door, and hoped Bramble wouldn't want her to personally introduce him to anyone else in the community. She was already disliked by the villagers, she didn't need to be hated by them too. Thankfully, after a last walk around the village Green, Bramble suggested they go up to the manor house to see how far along the forensics team were, and whether they had unearthed anything else of interest. Flora released a sigh of relief. At least up at The Rise, no one would see her helping the police with their enquiries. She felt very torn – her natural curiosity and desire to be involved and kept in the loop was fighting with the knowledge that she was possibly jeopardising her future happiness in the village even further. As much as Flora enjoyed Bramble's company, she wondered what it would cost her in the long run. She was therefore pre-occupied on the walk up to the manor house, and Bramble had to try several times before he got her attention.

"Flora?" he sounded impatient now.

"Sorry, Detective, I was in my own little world," Flora felt herself blushing again.

"That's quite alright, Flora, I assume you have not been party to many potential murder investigations?"

When he said the word in such a forthright manner, in the cold light of day, it made Flora's hair on the back of her neck bristle. She realised she probably wasn't cut out to be an amateur sleuth, be it here or in any village.

Best stick to the romance novels.

"Ah, no, Detective Bramble, this is my first actually.
Can you tell?" she tried to ask the question jokily, but
the way Flora was wringing her hands together belied
the anxiety which was rippling just under the surface
of her outward demeanour. She suddenly wished she
was back at home with Reggie.

"And who is that?" Flora realised she had zoned out
again, and that Bramble was asking her another
question. He pointed off to the side of them, in the
direction of a bench amongst some freshly-trimmed
hedges. There, snoring away, was Billy Northcote.

"Oh, that's the gardener. Well, former gardener, he
seems to work for free now," Flora shrugged her
shoulders, trying to emphasize that she really didn't
completely understand the man's logic either, "he's
older than he looks, but seems as fit as a fiddle. Was
quite friendly with Harry."

"Really? Seems he was almost the only one who was!
Let's have a quick word," Bramble walked in Billy's
direction before Flora had a chance to suggest they
leave the man to rest.

"Mr. Northcote? Mr. Northcote?" Bramble laid a gentle hand on Billy's shoulder. Were it not for the rumbling sounds of the man's snores, Flora would have been worried that he was no longer with them, so deep was his sleep.

"Aye?" Billy rubbed a grubby hand across his face and sat straighter. Soil stuck to the man's fingers, and was now smeared across the bridge of his nose.

"It's just me, Flora, from the tearoom," she said softly, not wanting to startle the man, "with a detective. He's come to look into what happened to Harry."

At the mention of his former employer, Billy finally woke up properly, standing shakily and raising a hand out to Bramble.

"William Northcote, pleased to meet you."

"Adam Bramble, likewise. Please take a seat Mr. Northcote, these are merely informal enquiries at present."

Billy sat on the bench, and Flora decided to take the seat next to him. Her feet were already sore in the wedge heels she was wearing, and she had not slept well the night before, visions of scones and typewriters and blackmail notes swirling in her mind. Even Reggie had become sick of her tossing and turning, squawking a sharp, "Settle down woman!" when she disturbed his slumber for the umpteenth time with another trip to the bathroom.

"So, Mr. Northcote," Bramble began.

"Billy, please."

"Billy, thank you. So, Billy, what can you tell me of the day your former employer passed away. I believe you were the one to find the, ah, body?"

"Yes, sir, and as I said to Mrs Miller here, right shocked I was!"

"I can imagine. Stays with a man, it does, finding a person like that," Bramble replied with empathy, his voice low and understanding. Flora felt grateful to him for the kindness in his tone.

"It does, sir, it does. The doctor said he choked, but there was no food nor an empty plate nearby," he may be getting on in years, but Billy was clearly still as sharp as a tack, "I wished I had come in from working on those bushes sooner, I did."

"Indeed," Bramble made more notes in his notepad, "and earlier in the day, tell me, did you see anybody about while you were trimming the hedges out front?"

"I did, sir, I saw Farmer Houghton, mighty angry he were, and I heard some woman in clip cloppy heels after that. Oh, and the teacher, whatshisname came up first."

Bramble looked to Flora to clarify. Her stomach felt like a lead weight had just settled as she realised she had completely left Phil out of her list the previous evening. Was it her sub-conscious trying to keep him out of the investigation, or merely an innocent error on her part? She felt suddenly flustered, and didn't want to look up into Bramble's eyes. Instead, she looked at Billy and said, "Phil Drayford, one of two teachers at the local primary school."

"I see," Bramble raised an eyebrow but said nothing further, simply scribbled the name into his pad.

After a few more minutes with Billy, Bramble made their excuses and they trundled the short way up the drive to the big house at the top. Flora felt that it loomed over her, a huge, stone weight on her shoulders, and she immediately took Bramble to the side of the building, where the door had been propped open by the scientific teams. Flora felt a sudden urge to rush back to the coach house and curl up on her bed. She had promised herself after her marriage ended that she would no longer bury her head in the sand, she would face everything head-on. However, she hadn't envisaged taking part in a murder investigation when she had made herself that vow. Taking a deep breath, she stepped from the sunlight into the darkness once again.

TWENTY-SIX

Bramble's keen eyes scanned the hallway as they walked to the front of the house, where they could hear the hum of the forensics team busy in the sitting room.

"Wow, this is not what I expected," Bramble said as they entered, his eyes round as saucers, "your predecessor really let the place go, didn't he," he gestured to the piles of papers, stained and damaged furniture and filthy floor.

"He did, I'm afraid," Flora whispered, uncomfortable around the three people in hazmat suits.

"Have you found anything, Bob?" Bramble asked the man closest to him.

"Well, Detective, there's a lot to go through, and many,

ah," he looked at Flora warily, "things that are quite unhygienic," he added sombrely.

"Yes, I'm sure the lab will get a lot of cultures from this place," Bramble almost joked, but there was no mirth in his tone.

"Why don't you take me to the other room, the one where you found the papers?" he asked Flora, gently leading her by the elbow out of the area. Clearly, her silence and discomfort was not lost on him.

"Thank you," Flora whispered as they headed back down the dimly lit hallway and into the study.

Bramble sighed audibly as he saw the piles of paper stacked haphazardly, and then actually groaned when he saw those that Flora had accidently tipped over the floor earlier in the week, "Please don't tell me we have to go through all these?" he asked.

"No, no, the place with the important paperwork, the stuff which seems to matter, is very well organised, actually."

"Thank goodness, oh watch your step there!" Bramble reached out and caught Flora's arm as she was about to walk into the dratted bucket again.

Why can I never remember it's there? She asked herself

woefully, though outwardly Flora simply said, "damp ceiling," and cast her eyes upward.

"Damp is not the word, Flora, that looks like it could come down at any time," Bramble angled her away from the area, where the ceiling was now filled with large, jiggling water bubbles which dripped a constant stream into and around the bucket waiting below.

Flora asked Bramble to remain where he was, as she skirted around the soggy rug and made her way to the large mantle. Grabbing hold of the candlestick, she pulled it sharply to the left. The grinding noise which filled the room was evidence that she had succeeded in opening the secret door again, and Flora heard Bramble's sharp intake of breath behind her.

"Well I never," he exclaimed, "it's like something from an old black and white thriller!" he moved slowly into the smaller space, all exactly as Flora had left it.

"It is quite something," she replied, joining him.

"So, has it stayed completely untouched since Harold then?" the awe was apparent in Bramble's voice still.

"Yes, apart from the things I removed and gave straight to you. I replaced the files in their original positions."

"Excellent. Well, we'll need a team in to go through all this," Bramble was starting to sound excited now. Like the hound that has caught a whiff of the chase.

"I would rather, well, I do need to know myself what is here if I am to run the estate," Flora said, trying to sound firm. In truth, she did not relish the prospect of going through the room alone, worried what other skeletons might appear out of this particular closet.

"Hmm," Bramble appeared to be contemplating this, "well, we need to do a thorough search in here, like with the front room I'm afraid, but how about we pass any paperwork to you once it's been gone over. In stages, as we do it. I could drop them at the coach house – I realise with the tearoom you can't spend the next few days glued to this spot."

"Indeed," nor did Flora wish to, she knew, "thank you, Detective."

Bramble looked as though he was itching to get stuck into the job now, though he planted his hands firmly in his pockets with his notepad and pen and said instead, "So, how about we visit that tearoom of yours? I think we both deserve a cuppa!"

"That sounds like a fine plan," Flora let out the breath she hadn't realised she was holding, happy to be heading out of this oppressive place once more.

Tanya welcomed them with a smile and a wave from the counter, where she was busy taking payment from what looked to be a group of hikers. Flora was glad that there'd been some business, it being the weekend and what should be her busiest day of the week.

"Thank you so much for helping me out at such short notice," Flora gave Tanya a hug, "Please let me introduce Detective Adam Bramble. Bramble this is Tanya Hughes, whose husband is the local policeman."

I'm doing it now, Flora thought to herself, *introducing people by their spouse's position in the village.* It irked her.

"Indeed, a pleasure to meet you," Bramble said, extending his hand, "I will have to pop along and speak with your husband shortly."

Tanya seemed to flush under the attention, and simply nodded in response. Turning from Bramble to Flora she changed the subject quickly, "So, no Reggie today? Have you clipped his naughty wings?" she laughed, but the sound was stilted.

"Ah no, we didn't come straight here," Flora didn't elaborate, "but we are desperate for a hot drink now!"

"Yes, policing is thirsty work," Bramble tipped a wink at them both, before taking a seat at the nearest table. Both women set to work at the coffee machine looking hot and flustered, though perhaps not for the same reasons.

TWENTY-SEVEN

After saying goodbye to Tanya, who rushed off soon after they arrived, and then chatting with Bramble over coffee, it was past lunchtime when Flora was alone again. She quickly locked up the tearoom for a few minutes and hurried home to collect Reggie, worried that he would have become lonely after several hours left to his own devices. As she returned to the café, with him flying ahead, a very well-dressed woman waited by the door. Flora rushed the last few steps, embarrassed that a customer should find the place closed in the middle of the day. To her dismay however, when the visitor looked up at their approach, she turned out to be no other than Edwina Edwards. She had an impatient expression and glared at Flora as she got nearer. Flora wished she had taken a moment at home to brush her hair, or at least had kept on the wedges which she had since changed for a much more boring pair of flats. Compared to the other woman, with her striking red lipstick and dress of the same colour, with co-ordinating green scarf, Flora felt positively dowdy.

She plastered a smile on her face, though, as any good shop owner does, and was about to greet the woman, when Reggie also clocked their guest.

"Stuffy old trout! Stuffy old trout!" he shrieked, swooping at her from above, and causing Mrs. Edwards to protect her head with her prim green handbag.

"Agh! You disgusting bird! You filthy fleabag!" she shouted up at the sky from beneath the temporary shelter of her bag. The woman's words had no effect on Reggie, however, save perhaps egging him on to greater squawking and to dive bombing Mrs. Edwards from an even greater height.

"I am so sorry," Flora stepped between the furious woman and the door, unlocking it quickly so that they could duck inside. Of course, Reggie followed where Flora went, and so the two women were now trapped inside with his shrieking attack.

"Enough, Reginald!" Flora said sternly, hoping that the

bird would recognise the more formal use of his name.
He stopped for a moment, feathers quaking, resting on
a table next to where Edwina Edwards cowered by the
doorway. Flora seized the lull in activity as her chance
to begin the slow process of making up for her
feathered companion's behaviour. She helped a shaken
Mrs. Edwards up by the elbow and escorted her to a
table at the front of the tearoom, right beside the
counter. When Reggie looked like he was about to
follow, Flora uttered a strict, "Perch now or home,"
which seemed to finally put the bird in his place, and
he sulked back to his metal stand in the back corner.

" I cannot begin to tell you how sorry I am," Flora
began, only to be cut off by the scathing tone of her
guest.

"Enough apologising. The bird should be shot, that is
all there is to it. You would be well advised to call the
vet and have him dispose of the animal."

"Well, really, I don't think…"

"He is a menace, and was Harold Baker's sidekick. For
that reason alone, he doesn't deserve to liv…"

"Well, Mrs. Edwards, I was about to offer you a cup of
sweet tea to calm your nerves – which are evidently
shredded. You can't possibly know what you are

saying. Reggie is an animal, a living creature. Anyway, as you are at such a discomfort perhaps it is better if you leave!"

"Well I never! I have never been spoken to in such a manner. My husband is the doctor in this community, you know! A man of status and…"

"But it is not your husband to whom I am speaking now, is it? Was there even a purpose to your visit, Edwina?" Flora deliberately used the familiar term of the woman's first name, as she didn't seem to be able to help herself, she simply had to goad the stuck up creature further.

"I had come to extend to you an invite to join us in the Women's Institute. We were even prepared to overlook your shocking lack of baking skills!"

"Well, as much as I would have no doubt managed to tolerate being a member of that hallowed institution, I'm afraid I would have had to decline anyway, given that I am now owner of the whole Baker Estate and all the properties that entails. I am a very busy woman." Flora enunciated the last words clearly.

For the first time, Edwina's face blanched and she stuttered over her words. Sensing an advantage, Flora pushed on, "Indeed, my time is even more taken up currently as I am assisting the police in their investigation into Harold Baker's death."

Edwina stood up abruptly and the chair clattered beneath her. She raised a shaking hand to fix an invisible strand of hair which she must have assumed had escaped from her stiff bob, and placed her bag firmly on her shoulder.

"I had heard that you had been seen in the village with a strange man, and that there had been police going door to door, but I scarcely believed it when Ray Dodds told me he suspected it had to do with that man, Harold Baker," Edwina practically spat the name, as she inched backwards towards the door, "I had thought we were rid of the likes of him, but I see now I was mistaken."

Flora, unsure what to reply to that remark, thought only to get the rude woman out of the building as quickly as possible. She rushed past Edwina and held the door wide open for her. As the woman was about to walk out, however, inspiration struck and Flora said, "As owner of the estate, lady of the manor if you will, I will of course be taking up my rightful place as head judge at this year's village fete. You do bake, do you not Mrs. Edwards? I imagine… scones are your thing?" It was a shot in the dark, but the bullet hit its mark perfectly. If it was possible, Edwina turned an even paler shade of white and rushed away without another word, her hand gripping the silk scarf at her neck tightly.

Flora knew she had made an enemy, but in this moment she did not care. The woman's reactions had given her much food for thought, and Flora intended to mull them over whilst enjoying some tea and cake. After all, with all of the calories she must have expended touring the village earlier, a small slice wouldn't hurt!

TWENTY-EIGHT

After a thankfully uneventful evening, Flora went to
bed early, exhausted from both the day's events, and
her lack of sleep the night before. She was glad to have
checked the calendar in her phone before retiring for
the evening, as it reminded her that she had accepted
an invitation to have Sunday lunch with Betty Lafferty
the following day. Flora was looking forward to
enjoying the woman's easy conversation and good
humour. First, though, she had to get through the
weekly church service.

It was a chilly, drizzly day which reminded Flora more
of the onset of autumn than of mid-summer. She
pulled her smart jacket around her tightly as she
walked the path up to the large, wooden doors of the
church, dismayed when she saw the vicar waiting

---

there to greet arrivals, and no-one in the vicinity to dilute their conversation. Flora took a deep breath and ploughed onward. Thankfully, out of the corner of her eye, she spotted a black car pull up by the kerb and a familiar, tall figure un-bend himself out of the driver's door. Bramble. Flora couldn't remember a time recently when she had been more relieved to see an acquaintance.

"Detective Bramble," she greeted the raincoat-clad man, who immediately offered her his arm to link with hers.

"Mrs. Miller, thank goodness I have met you, I did not want to walk in there unaccompanied. Despite all my years of policing, small rural communities like this, where strangers are often shunned, are my idea of social hell!"

"Quite," Flora agreed merrily, a cheery smile on her lips, as they approached the waiting vicar.

"Good morning," the way Reverend Wright spat the words at them, suggested he wished Flora and Bramble anything but a good morning. Flora smiled to herself as she simply nodded to the dislikeable man. The vicar's gaze, however, was fixed on Bramble.

"I don't believe we have met," he snapped out.

"Detective Bramble, Northumberland Police," Bramble smiled, but it was a cooler expression than the genuine smile which he had bestowed on Flora only a few moments before.

"Indeed, we should talk about the graffiti on local monuments by a small group of uncouth youths," the vicar smiled and Flora found the effect to be rather unpleasant, his calculating eyes not deviating from Bramble's face.

"I'm afraid I have much more pressing matters in the village at the moment. But for today, I am off the clock," Bramble walked straight into the church then, Flora still on his arm, leaving the vicar open-mouthed.

"What a strange man to be parish vicar," Bramble whispered in Flora's ear as they sat together in a middle pew, "he fair gave me the creeps!"

Flora tried to stifle the giggle that bubbled up quickly, "Quite, my thoughts exactly," she whispered back. From this distance she could smell Bramble's fresh scent of soap and some kind of wood spice. She tried not to focus on the feeling of his stubble rubbing against her cheek as he whispered in her ear.

"So, you can give me the low down on everyone after the service," Bramble added, and Flora tried hard to concentrate on his words. She noticed, with a small feeling of guilt, that Phil had turned from his position two pews ahead of them, and was gazing at her with a mixture of sadness and annoyance. Flora didn't have time to pay him much heed, though, as in the next minute the vicar himself rushed up the aisle and onto the pulpit, signalling the start of the service.

After what seemed to be an interminably long sermon, they finally reached the end of service prayers. Flora kept her eyes open when everyone bowed their heads, and was surprised when Phil turned to look at her. She met his eyes and mouthed "hi," but received no smile in return. He was clearly miffed, though whether it was the presence of Bramble by her side, or something else, Flora couldn't tell. As the villagers filed out at the end of the service, Betty came rushing up to them, her smile welcoming and hearty.

"Flora, lass, you haven't forgotten my invitation, have you?"

"Certainly not, Mrs. Lafferty, I have been looking forward to it!"

"Excellent, but call me Betty, no need to stand on ceremony. I hope you don't mind, I've invited Harry

Bentley along too," Betty's eyes shone brightly when she mentioned the man's name, and Flora suppressed a grin, "And who is this handsome man by your side?" Betty turned her attention to Bramble, who was scanning the departing congregation.

"Oh, this is Detective Bramble, though he is off duty today," Flora said, wishing Phil hadn't chosen that moment to walk past and hear Bramble described as 'handsome'. It was true though, he was rather good looking!

Bramble turned and introduced himself to Betty, kissing her outstretched hand instead of shaking it. Betty giggled like a schoolgirl, and Flora knew immediately that he had won over the older woman.

"Detective, we are only three for lunch, but I have cooked easily enough for four. Would you like to join us, unless your wife is waiting for you at home?" Betty asked casually, casting a sly sideways glance at Flora. Subtle as a brick. Or as a parrot, Flora thought. She had the distinct impression Betty was playing matchmaker, but said nothing to deter Bramble from accepting. It would be nice to share a meal with the man and get to know him better. Of course, though he was not at work today, he was no doubt here to subtly further his enquiries. Either way, Flora was happy for his company.

Bramble accepted Betty's invitation to Sunday lunch with gusto, declaring that regrettably no Mrs. Bramble existed. Flora tried to ignore the warm feeling she got at this knowledge. The three of them made their way to the front lawn outside the church to look for Harry, who had skipped the service and was meeting them there. Flora was relieved when the vicar refrained from coming over to them as they waited, though she caught him looking in Bramble's direction a few times, a worried look on his face.

TWENTY-NINE

Betty's cottage was as charming as Flora had imagined it to be. She had clearly left the roast chicken cooking in the oven while she was at church, as the smell as they entered the sitting room was delicious. A small, yappy dog greeted them excitedly, clearly recognising Harry, whom it jumped up at, sniffing the pocket of Harry's suit jacket. Well prepared, Harry produced a dog biscuit, and the tiny terrier raced with its treasure back to a large cushion in front of the fire, which was already covered in dog hairs.

"Shall I get the fire going, Betty?" Harry asked, as the older woman rushed straight into the small back kitchen to check on the meal.

"Aye, that'll be grand, Harry love," Betty called back, as Bramble and Flora hovered awkwardly in the tiny hallway.

"Now, don't you be standing on ceremony," Betty appeared again, minus her hat that she'd worn for church, and tying an apron around her ample waist, "Take your coats off and have a seat at the table there."

Moving further into the sitting room, Flora saw a small dining table, set for three, with dark wooden chairs and a brightly embroidered tablecloth. Unlike the similar scene at the vicarage from a few days ago, Betty's was the epitome of homely comfort.

"Here you go," Betty handed Bramble the cutlery and place mat for an extra setting, "Make yourself useful, young man!"

Bramble smiled and immediately went to do her bidding. He looked up as he was rearranging the table, at Flora who had taken a seat on the small chintzy settee, and gave her a surreptitious wink. Flora blushed and smiled back at him, until Harry rose from his place at the fireplace, the coal fire lit with a small flame.

"It'll be roaring away soon enough," he said, giving the dog a tickle behind the ear and coming to sit beside Flora, "have you met Tina here?" he indicated the furry companion.

"No, she's very sweet," Flora replied politely, though in truth she wasn't used to dogs, and felt startled every time one barked nearby.

"So," Harry said, his voice lowered now, "is everything okay, up at the manor? I see the police have been round the village," he raised a curious eyebrow.

I'll call you later and fill you in," Flora whispered back, as Bramble came to join them. The two men had been introduced for the first time on the walk from the church, but seemed to immediately hit it off. Flora hadn't seen Harry be awkward or unfriendly to anyone, and the detective was no exception. Flora left the two men chatting as she went into the kitchen to offer Betty her help. The small galley-shaped room was cosy, with yellow frilly curtains at the back window, which overlooked a small garden overflowing with flowers in pots of every size and colour.

"If you could stir the gravy, that would be lovely," Betty said, taking the chicken from the oven before draining the potatoes to make the mash. She chatted away as she worked, enquiring as to where Flora had found such a handsome man as Bramble. Flora said he was in the village looking into Harold's death – she saw no reason to keep that fact a secret – and then turned the conversation to ask how long Betty and

Harry had known each other.

"Ah, we go way back to our youth. I think I was in my twenties and had just had my first son when Harry and his new wife arrived in Baker's Rise" Betty said, blushing, "though he and I didn't become firm, ah, friends till many years later when we were both widowed. I had a different childhood sweetheart, you see – Harold Baker actually."

"Really?" Flora couldn't keep the shock from her voice. From what she'd been told of Harold, she couldn't imagine a woman as sweet as Betty being interested in him, "but he never married?"

"No lass, he had an eye for the women – his whole life in fact – and when he was young he was a handful, to be sure. We courted for a while, until he strayed. I was heartbroken for a few months, but then I met my husband and that, as they say, is history."

"And he never got as far as the alter with anyone?" Flora asked, helping Betty to plate up the food, eyeing the huge Yorkshire puddings hungrily.

"No, lass, his wandering hands got him in trouble far too often. Broke up every relationship he had, from what I heard on the village grapevine. Always had a soft spot for me, though. I think that's why he chose my scone as the winner at the fete last year. I know it wasn't really the best, but it was apple and cinnamon, which I remembered was his favourite. It was my last year as leader of the WI, so I think that and the nostalgia played a part in him giving me the rosette for first place."

"Oh, I'm sure your win was rightly deserved Betty, you're just too modest!" Flora said, deliberately not asking about the kerfuffle which Tanya had mentioned had happened at that time, nor the fact that she knew Enid Wright's nose had been put sorely out of joint by having to live with the apparent embarrassment of coming second place.

"Well, Harry there has never had any complaints," Flora said, giggling lightly, as they carried the food out to the men who were waiting at the table. Flora wondered if they were still referring to scones, as Harry winked overtly at Betty and she flushed red in response.

"Tuck in dears," Betty invited, then with a sparkle in her eye, said to Flora, "I heard you refused Edwina Edward's offer to join the ranks of the WI?"

"Well, yes," Flora smiled at the memory, "she didn't really couch the invite in very complimentary terms, though it was memorable!" Bramble looked her way and cocked an eyebrow but said nothing as Flora continued, "I did mention that I'll be the one judging at the fete this year, though, since the honour always goes to the owner of The Rise, and that shut her up pretty quickly!" Betty chuckled, and Flora saw the little flare of hope alight in the woman's eyes, she knew she would have to be careful not to show favouritism when the time came.

The women chatted more about the Women's Institute, and where its fame for jam and baking originated from, and then talk turned to village life, and the hilarity of the doctor and his wife insisting on winning the pub quiz every single week. There was a lot of laughter, spurred on by the bottle of expensive Chateauneuf-du-Pape which Harry had brought and which flowed well throughout the meal. Bramble stuck to elderflower water as he was driving back to his home outside Morpeth afterwards.

Topped off with one of Betty's home-made lemon meringue pies, it was the perfect Sunday lunch, and just what Flora had needed to take her mind off the rather more sombre events of recent days.

THIRTY

When Bramble drove her the short way back to the coach house at half past three, Flora was acutely aware of how close she was sitting to him in his small car. His hand brushed her thigh every time he changed gears, and she willed her heart to slow down, chastising herself inwardly for her ridiculous reactions. A woman of her age should not be feeling all heady over the proximity of a man. Especially a woman who was recently divorced and not looking for a relationship. Flora had just invited Bramble in for a coffee as they rounded the driveway to her home, when she saw another vehicle pulled up ahead of them. As Bramble turned off the engine, Phil emerged from his parked car, a stack of brown and black papers in his arms.

"Ah, I'll take a rain check, " Bramble said politely, "I'll be speaking to Mr. Drayford more formally tomorrow as part of the investigation."

And there she was, back down to earth with a crash. *Why does this keep happening?* Flora wondered, as she said a reluctant goodbye to Bramble and watched him reverse away, before she greeted Phil with as much of a smile as she could muster. Every time she began to feel happy, her bubble was burst and she was brought back to reality. *I really must get a better grip on my emotions. It's like being on a rollercoaster!* She thought, before feeling a bit guilty for her dwindling spirits, as Phil had been nothing but a friend to her.

"Sorry, Flora, I did text to say I was coming round, rambling trip finished early," he shuffled awkwardly from foot to foot.

"I was having lunch at Betty's and must've left my phone at home this morning," Flora spoke over her shoulder as she unlocked the door and was greeted with a cloud of green feathers hurtling towards her.

"Been a while, been a while," Reggie chirped, flapping in her face and then settling on Flora's shoulder, from where he spied Phil coming in behind her.

"Not that jerk! Not that jerk!" Reggie squawked, making Flora flush with embarrassment. He made it sound like he was repeating her words, and not those of Harold.

"Reggie, enough or cage!" Flora used the only threat which she had found to work with the bird, "I'm so sorry Phil, he has an... eclectic vocabulary."

"That's one word for it," Phil muttered, not very graciously, as he dumped the contents of his arms onto the coffee table in the sitting room, tripping over a box of Flora's expensive Italian shoes in his haste to escape Reggie's glare.

As the parrot settled on his perch in the corner of the room, Flora turned on the heating, because despite it being summer there was a definite chill in the air.

Phil began talking quickly, as if unsure of himself, "So, these are some of the photos from the storeroom at the school. I know you wanted to go through them and pick the ones to go on display at the tearoom this week, ready for your big opening event next Saturday. Then I thought we could have a second pile of extras to be added to the stall at the village fete next month, it'll be fun for the locals to look for their classmates from years back. We could make copies and sell them on the stall..."

"Phil," Flora laid her hand on his arm gently, "how about I get us some chamomile tea?" The poor man certainly needed to something to calm him, his nerves were clearly frayed, and Flora wondered if it wasn't something more than Reggie which had put him so ill at ease.

"Yes, thank you, Flora, that would be lovely," he sighed and knelt on the floor beside the table, his silence speaking almost as clearly as his words just had.

Flora made her way into the kitchen and filled the kettle, hearing Phil follow her a moment later.

"So, that was the detective you were with?" Phil asked, apparently aiming for a nonchalant tone, but actually just sounding strained, "do you think it was murder? Are they making any progress narrowing down a list of suspects?"

"It was. Have you met him yet?" Flora eyed Phil from the corner of her eye as she deliberately answered only his first question. A more ill-at-ease man she would struggle to find in this sleepy village right now.

"No, just one of the uniformed officers who came to my door. I imagine he'll get around to me soon though. I was… I was up at Harold's on the day he died," Phil stared resolutely at the floor, avoiding Flora's eyes.

She didn't want to tell him that she knew this, that Billy Northcote had already filled her in on the comings and goings at The Rise that fateful morning, so she simply nodded and added two teabags to the pretty china cups.

Phil rushed on, "We didn't have a very good history, Baker and I," his words caught in his throat then and Flora stopped what she was doing and turned completely to face the man.

"Phil," she said, resting her hand on his arm, "are you worried you'll be implicated in Harold's death? Being there that morning is just circumstantial, unless there's anything else more damning...?" Flora knew she was pushing for information now – information which she should let the police discover – but something in her couldn't help but be curious. Besides, what if she were to unravel the mystery herself? Wouldn't Bramble think even more highly of her then? He would surely shower her in praise.

"Well, I, well, I," Phil spluttered, raking one hand through his hair and using the other to squeeze the nape of his neck, "I had better be going. The cat, ah, needs feeding!" It was a feeble excuse, and he obviously knew it, for Phil turned a deep shade of red and before Flora had time to process it, he was out the front door and away.

"Well, Reggie," Flora said, after locking the door behind her escaping guest and taking a cup of chamomile tea into the sitting room, "what are we to make of that then?"

"Put your feet up!" Reggie chirped, as if he was happy that it was finally just the two of them again. Flora eyed the stacks of aging photographs on her coffee table. Somehow, they didn't seem out of place amongst her boxes of clothes and accessories. She really couldn't be bothered to start sorting them now. The wine from lunchtime was making her sleepy, so she decided they would have to wait till tomorrow evening after work. Besides, Phil had bolted, so why should she be left with it all to do?

No, she would enjoy her cuppa, and then maybe start on her romance novel, Flora decided, as even then her head began to droop and she was soon snoring lightly.

THIRTY-ONE

For perhaps the first time since arriving at the village, Flora felt completely refreshed when she awoke the next morning. She had spent a pleasant evening outlining her novel and then taking a long soak in the bath, before an early night with a book, and now she was raring to go again. At the tearoom before George Jones arrived with the bakery goods, Flora had put all of the school photos into a large bin bag which she had lugged down the path with her. She had decided that she would sort through them when there were lulls in the day – of which there would be many, she was sure. Never mind, word of her little event this Saturday had started to spread, so Betty had assured her yesterday, and people were looking forward to the free tea and cake on offer. Hopefully business would build steadily after the locals had a chance to try the place out.

There was no postal delivery that morning, not that she minded avoiding the rude mailman, so Flora was sitting with a latte and a large smile on her face when Detective Bramble arrived. The smile had not a little to do with the plate of warm scones sitting on the counter, not perfect, but sellable nonetheless! Indeed, Flora may even have sampled one or two herself to make sure they were fit for consumption!

"Somebody new! Somebody new!" Reggie chirped as Bramble entered to the sound of the bell tinkling on the tearoom door, though for once the bird remained where he was on his perch.

"Hush Reggie! Good morning, Detective!" Flora smiled at the man and received a warm expression in return.

"Good morning, Flora. I have been busy already and thought I'd stop in for a refreshment!"

Flora desperately wanted to quiz the man on any developments, but forced herself to play hostess first, taking his order and preparing the double-shot espresso which the detective requested. She then set his small cup on the table, along with the plate of scones, which she delivered with a flourish.

"Baked fresh this morning, Detective," Flora said, only now her confidence faltering at the thought of someone else tasting her creations. She swallowed it down. If the Tearoom on The Rise was going to succeed, Flora would need to show the same confidence she had with her career in the City for all those years.

"Well, don't they look a picture," Bramble said, winking at Flora, who felt the heat rise up her neck and into her face. She suddenly wished she weren't wearing her cardigan, as the warmth in the room had just jumped several notches.

"Thank you, I'll get you some clotted cream and jam," Flora busied herself in an attempt to hide her pleasure at his words. When she finally came to sit with the detective, at his invitation, Flora felt much calmer.

"So, have you had a fruitful morning so far?" Flora tried to make the enquiry seem innocent, when in reality she was desperate for any more clues.

"Well, it is only ten o'clock," Bramble chuckled, "but I have spoken to a few people, yes."

"Oh?" Flora looked down at her cup.

"I saw the postman, Mr. Stanton is it?" Bramble brought out the little notebook and turned to the most recent page, "He was a revelation. Started firing information at me before I could even ask the questions. People with a guilty conscience tend to do that, you see."

"Do they really?" Flora was dismayed when her mind immediately returned to her brief conversation with Phil the previous day.

"Indeed. I'll need to take an official statement at the station of course, but it turns out your local postie was taking a nice little backhander from old Harold up there, to hand deliver some letters when he was on his normal rounds."

"Really?" Flora felt a sense of excitement and anticipation build in her. Were these letters the threatening notes made from the newspaper cuttings she had found? The ones that would confirm Harold had been a blackmailer?

"Yes, and well, I suppose since you know all the details anyway, there's no harm in me telling you – in full confidence of course…"

"Of course!"

"…that Joe Stanton was delivering occasional blackmail notes for Harold. For a hefty fee, I might add. You were right, he is looking into some of the post, he said the letters 'pop open' by themselves and he reseals them out of the goodness of his heart, that he can't help it if the envelopes are a bit see through and he catches a glimpse of what's inside! What a load of cra... rubbish!"

"Goodness me! I suspected but I didn't like to believe it. Did he say who he hand-delivered the messages to?"

Bramble seemed to think for a minute, before coming to an internal decision, "Aye, he did mention some names actually," he lowered his voice even further, so that Flora had to move her ear close to his mouth to hear, despite them being the only two in the place, "he said that Pat Hughes, your local constable got one, and the doctor..."

"Doctor Edwards?"

"Yep, then one for the vicar..."

"The Reverend Wright?" Flora was starting to sound and feel like a parrot herself now!

"Indeed, and then that teacher that we saw outside your place yesterday, Mr. Drayford."

Flora's stomach sank a little at this last piece of information, but she allowed nothing to show in her face, "Goodness me, that's quite a list!"

"Isn't it just. Apparently there were more, too, but those were the ones that sprang to mind when Stanton was put on the spot. We will have to speak to PC Hughes at the station, as more of an internal investigation, but the other three are on my list for this morning. I'm just waiting for Detective Blackett to join me and then we can get to it." Bramble started tucking into his scone then, making appreciative noises as he ate, but Flora's mind was whirling too fast to appreciate the compliment. Should she warn Phil? No, she had been told this in confidence. Besides, he had seemed shifty enough yesterday, let the police make of it what they would.

"Thank you, Flora," Bramble rose, downing his espresso in one huge gulp, as a car was heard pulling up outside, "There's Blackett. I won't inflict his bad humour on you, he's never great on Mondays!"

He didn't seem in a good mood the other day either! Flora thought, not able to imagine the sombre man in anything but a grumpy mood, though she simply said, "Do come back and fill me in on any developments, Detective!" the hope in her voice plain to hear.

"Will do, Flora," Bramble spoke over his shoulder as he left the tearoom, and the place seemed bigger and colder somehow in his wake.

Flora had little time to sit and ponder these latest developments, however, as the bell tinkled at eleven on the dot and Betty arrived, her small terrier in tow.

"Is she allowed in," Betty asked, poking her head around the door.

Flora took a moment to think about it. She hadn't considered allowing dogs in before now, but since a lot of ramblers had dogs with them, and it was hardly as if the tearoom was busy, she said yes, thinking she could always reconsider her decision at a later date.

"Perfect, thanks lass, I'm fair parched, I am," Betty said as she came in, little Tina dragged along behind her on a pink leash.

"Tina the Terror! Tina the Terror!" Reggie began squawking, flapping his wings and flying up with an eye to begin divebombing the little dog.

"Reggie!" Flora shouted horrified, before she wondered if he was simply frightened. She walked across to the perch, passing Betty who had picked Tina up and was rushing for a table at the front near the counter. Flora reached the bird and lifted her arm for him to alight on it. Sure enough, Reggie came straight to her and perched on Flora's shoulder, nestling into the crook of her neck and chirping softly.

"Cosy now," Reggie chirped, and Flora felt a wave of happiness surge through her. Perhaps having a pet wasn't so bad after all.

THIRTY-TWO

After a lovely chat with Betty, who had left after an hour or so, Flora cleared up and tried to pinpoint why she was suddenly feeling so on edge. It wasn't because of Reggie, as he had settled down once little Tina was safely ensconced under the table and out of view. It wasn't Betty herself, as she had been great company as always. No, there was something else niggling her. After a few minutes of focused self-analysis, Flora realised what it was – she was anxious to hear what else Bramble had found. Perhaps she could go for a walk in the village, just to stretch her legs of course, and see if she could spot him? Deciding that she could afford to lock up for an hour, Flora seized the opportunity, and five minutes later she was striding down the driveway towards the main street of the village.

Whether it was by fate or chance, Flora did not have to walk far before she spotted Bramble, emerging from The Bun in the Oven, a distinctly sour look on his face.

"Flora!" he exclaimed when he saw her on the other side of the street, "Just a minute!" he rushed across the road, to where Flora hovered outside Baker's Rise Cuts and Dyes.

"Detective, I was just taking a midday stroll," Flora blushed at the thought of how easily the small fib glided off her tongue.

"That is very fortunate, as we've just finished speaking to Ray Dodds in the pub. He certainly didn't hide his dislike for Harold, so I don't think we've got anything to worry about there as far as the investigation goes. Wears his hatred for the deceased on his sleeve with pride, that one does!"

"Goodness," Flora wasn't sure what else to say.

"Anyway, Blackett's going back to Morpeth with Pat Hughes – a sorrier state for a police officer I never did see! And his wife, is she some kind of stage actress? She was definitely dressed... oddly."

"Tanya? Oh she's lovely, a bit quirky that's all. But as for Pat, well, I think you've already got the correct measure of the man. Though, I wonder if he's too lazy to go to the trouble of murdering anyone. And can he bake, I wonder? I doubt it!" Flora suppressed a shudder at the thought of the policeman.

"Can Tanya? Bake, I mean."

"I'm not sure to be honest, but I'd say no, as she was almost as clueless as me when Lily Houghton from the farm gave us both a lesson last week. She makes a mean coffee though!"

"Well, no rest for the wicked, I've got the vicarage and then the doctor's surgery on my list for today," Bramble paused for a moment, "you wouldn't have some time to spare to accompany me, would you? These being very informal enquiries, I don't think it's breaking protocol to have you with me. I'm just getting a feel for how people in the village regarded Harold at this stage."

"Of course!" a small thrill of exhilaration ran through Flora, though the thought of visiting the surgery and the vicarage wasn't necessarily a comfortable one.

It was the first time Flora had visited the doctor's surgery in Baker's Rise, and it reminded her of the fact that she really ought to register with the practice. Especially at her age, she thought morosely, you never know what might start to go wrong! Edwina Edwards sat at the reception desk looking as prim and proper as she always did. When she caught sight of Flora walking towards her, a distasteful look crossed her well-made-up face, though this was quickly hidden behind a mask of welcome when she spotted the man beside Flora.

"Mrs. Edwards?" Bramble asked as they reached the desk.

"Indeed, how can I be of help?" Edwina was all attentiveness now, though her gaze did not stray even once to Flora at his side.

"I'm Detective Inspector Bramble of the Northumberland Police, and I was wondering if we could have a quick word, with you and then with your husband, if we may?"

"Well, Doctor Edwards is very busy with surgery at the moment," a quick look around the empty waiting room told Flora this was unlikely to be the case, but she said nothing. Let Bramble deal with the woman.

"It really is a matter of great importance," the detective continued, his voice full of persuasion.

"Very well, come through to the office, and you can speak to me, while my husband finishes with his current patient."

"Thank you kindly, madam."

"Oh! Is she coming as well?" Edwina could not hide the shock from her voice when she saw Flora following Bramble into the room.

"Indeed, Mrs. Baker has been very helpful in providing information about the deceased," the detective's tone brooked no argument. Edwina Edwards let out a sigh of disapproval, though she said no more on the matter.

The office was a tiny room, with a desk, several filing cabinets and a large swivel chair. Edwina took the chair, leaving the two visitors to stand opposite her on the other side of the large desk.

"So, do you bake, Mrs. Edwards?" The question seemed to surprise Edwina, for she began to turn red, and all that came out of her mouth was a splutter.

Flora spoke up for the first time since entering the surgery, "Mrs. Edwards is the current chairperson of the Women's Institute."

"Indeed? Well, I imagine you can make a mean scone?" Bramble continued.

Edwina looked confused, clearly this was not the direction she had imagined their conversation taking, "I can indeed, Detective," she bit out.

"Excellent, and do you have a regular day of the week for baking?" Flora had filled the detective in on the idea that some women in the village baked regularly on certain days, whilst they were walking to the surgery. If they could determine who had baked on that fateful Saturday, the day of Harold's death, they could perhaps start to narrow things down.

"Well, yes, as it happens, I bake every Saturday morning," Edwina was completely red from the neck up now, a rather unbecoming shade of puce in fact. Flora tried not to take any pleasure in the other woman's discomfort, but it was hard, since she had been so rude to Flora the other day. Bramble was busy scribbling this new information into his small notepad.

At that moment, Doctor Edwards himself appeared from a door to the right, on the opposite wall to where they themselves had entered the room.

"That will be all for now, Mrs. Edwards… oh, one last question," Bramble caused the woman, who was beating a hasty retreat towards the door to the waiting room, to pause. "I presume you have access to the records of all the patients at this practice?"

"Well, yes, of course," Edwina stuttered, as if she felt she was somehow implicating herself further by the admission, and then rushed from the room, her usual composure distinctly absent. Bramble added this to his notes, as the doctor took the seat his wife had just vacated. In contrast to Mrs. Edwards, however, the man was a ghastly shade of white.

"Are you quite well, Sir?" Bramble asked kindly.

"Yes, just, well, you can imagine the viruses I'm constantly exposed to in this line of work," the doctor attempted a smile, which didn't reach the corners of his mouth, let alone his eyes.

"Well, yes," Bramble agreed, "now, I won't keep you long, Dr. Edwards, I just have a couple of questions about a death certificate you wrote last year. For the late Harold Baker."

The doctor shifted uncomfortably in his chair, avoiding making eye contact with either Flora or Bramble.

"Yes, I remember, how could I forget?" Edwards replied.

"Quite. Well, as you will recall, you stated the cause of death as choking. Can I ask why you chose that? Were there no indicators of any other potential cause?"

The doctor spluttered as if the words would not quite come out of his mouth. He loosened the tie around his neck and fidgeted with the pens arranged neatly on the desk. Eventually, he stood, looking Bramble straight in the eye, "There is always the chance of human error with these things, as I'm sure you'll understand, Detective. I always endeavour to be as accurate as possible in my conclusions, but without an autopsy one can never be one hundred percent sure on cause of death." Flora noticed the man's hands shaking, before he shoved them in his trouser pockets.

"Indeed," Bramble stood face to face with Edwards and did not step back under his glare, "thank you, doctor... oh, one last thing," again, as the physician was about to leave the room, Bramble called him back, "did you know your wife had been baking on the day in question?"

If it were possible, Flora thought she saw the man pale even further. He remained silent for too many seconds, seemingly weighing up his words, before eventually saying, "Yes, she bakes every Saturday."

"And did she leave the house at all after baking that day?" Bramble asked the question lightly, as if it carried no import at all.

"I do believe she may have dressed for an appointment in the village, yes," Edwards rushed out of the room as soon as the last word was out of his mouth. Flora had no police training, but she could tell when someone was acting guiltily when she saw them. Neither she nor Bramble spoke, however, until they were back outside and a good few steps along the pavement.

"Well, that was a revelation," Flora whispered.

"Maybe. Maybe not," Bramble said, shaking his head slightly, "I wonder if the good doctor simply saw the remains of the scone at the manor house when he knelt down beside the body, knew his wife had been baking before she then left the house, put two and two together and made five. Wrote choking as the cause of death in a misguided attempt to protect her. Perhaps she had been spouting off about Harold before she left. I'm not saying this is the case, just that there are more options than simply innocent or guilty."

"Fascinating," Flora said, as they walked towards the vicarage, "I would never have thought of it like that."

"Well, that's what twenty years in the job does for you, helps you see the bigger picture. Well, most of the time…" Bramble added.

He was certainly an interesting man, and clever too, but Flora got no hint of conceit from him. His humility only added to the detective's attractiveness as far as she was concerned!

THIRTY-THREE

Flora had to admit that she didn't relish the prospect of going back into the vicarage. Not after her somewhat spectacular exit the last time she was here. So, she hung back behind Bramble as he knocked on the heavy, iron lion's head door knocker and they waited in silence. At length, the door was opened by Enid Wright, bundled as usual in a thick, grey knit cardigan, her thinning grey hair scraped back into a bun.

"Can I help you?" she peered at Bramble over small spectacles that were perched on the end of her nose. It was when she caught sight of Flora, however, that the woman's impassive demeanour changed, and she pursed her lips and screwed up her eyes in an evident sign of displeasure.

"Yes, is the vicar at home please? Detective Adam Bramble and Mrs. Miller come to speak with him on a matter of some importance."

"He is. Come inside and I will let him know you are here," Enid scuttled off without waiting to see them into the hallway. Bramble turned to Flora, a small smile on his lips, and raised an eyebrow. She returned the expression, and they both smiled widely then. An unspoken message shared between them. Flora felt the warmth of the camaraderie down to her toes.

"Detective Bramble, do come in," the Reverend Wright stood at the doorway to what Flora assumed was his office. She noted that the invitation did not include her, but walked in ahead of Bramble when he stood to let her pass him first. *Such a thoughtful man!* There was no sign of Enid.

The vicar offered Bramble the guest seat in front of his desk, blatantly ignoring Flora, whilst he himself walked around to the large, comfy chair behind the table. Instead of taking the proffered seat, though, Bramble offered Flora the chair he had been shown and he himself stood behind her as she sat. Reverend Wright pursed his lips in evident displeasure, though said nothing. His eyes remained fixed on Bramble, completely blanking Flora.

"So, Detective, how can I help you? I imagine you are here because of the death of poor Harold? I heard that there were police asking questions the other day."

"Indeed. I will get straight to the point, Reverend, as I know you must be a busy man. I believe you were the recipient of some rather distressing mail in the months before the man's death?"

The vicar blanched and was subject to a sudden fit of coughing. Enid appeared out of nowhere with a glass of water, though Flora noted she and Bramble were not offered any refreshments. The couple clearly hoped it would be a flying visit.

When the vicar had composed himself, he spoke very quietly, certainly not his booming voice from the pulpit on Sundays, "I have no idea to what you are referring, Detective."

"Indeed? Very well. Then let me ask you this. You received funds from the tearoom, when it was open previously, towards your church roof fund?"

"I did, Mr. Baker generously gave half of his profits. It was an informal, mutual agreement, and such a generous donation to the cause."

"That is very generous indeed. Tell me, would you be amenable to having an architectural survey done of the church roof? Just to establish how much work needs doing and to estimate the costs of such? It could help your fundraising to have exact figures at hand."

The vicar reached up to his dog collar, as if it was suddenly too tight around his throat, and stood abruptly, "I have just remembered a prior engagement. You must excuse me Detective. Please do make an appointment if you wish to speak further," and with that he swept from the room, leaving Flora and Bramble in silence with no sound to break the thick tension in the air.

Back at the tearoom, to see that Reggie had unfortunately helped himself to one of her fruit scones from earlier and was looking very pleased with himself, Flora made a pot of tea for herself and another espresso for Bramble, before they sat down together.

"Are you sure you wouldn't like some sandwiches? Or a scone?" she asked, hopefully, as there was plenty that needed to be eaten before it ran out of date.

"No, thank you, Flora," Bramble patted his stomach ruefully, " I have to be careful now I'm in the grips of middle age!"

"Tell me about it!" Flora smiled, blushing at how open she could be with this man, "Now that it's just us, let me know what you were thinking at the vicarage!" Flora couldn't help herself, the curiosity always got the better of her.

"Ah well," Bramble put down his tiny coffee cup and smiled, "that was just a hunch. Don't you think it strange that Harold was giving away money from the tearoom? From what I've heard, that was not like him!"

"Quite out of character," Flora agreed, "so why did he do it?"

"Well, I'm just speculating, you understand, and we know this is just between us, but I have a feeling our good vicar over there must have had some dirt on Harold, and Harold made this regular 'donation' to keep him quiet. If Harold, in the course of amassing the files on everyone, found out something about the vicar to hold against him in return? Well, then the tearoom donation would no longer be necessary."

"Do you think it has to do with the church roof?"

"Quite so, the Reverend has been collecting for those

repairs since he arrived. I checked, and, as yet, nothing at all has been done to that roof."

"No building works whatsoever?"

"Nothing in the Church of England records, no, not even a single tile replaced. So, my thought is, where's the money gone?"

"My goodness! Will you report it?"

"Already done. The Reverend Wright should be getting a call from the Bishop in the next day or two, and an internal investigation will be launched. I've reported it to the Fraud Squad at the station too. We must keep that under our hats, though."

"Of course! Do you think Enid was aware of all this?"

"Quite possibly. She strikes me as being very astute."

"Is it enough motive to kill though?"

"Well, any motive, big or small, can be enough if the killer is so inclined. As for this, I'll have to do a bit more investigating! Speaking of investigating, thank you Flora but I must be getting back to the station to fill Blackett in on my findings and see what the state of play is with Pat Hughes."

"Of course, of course. Thank you for letting me tag

along."

"Any time," Bramble winked as he left, leaving Flora's emotions all aflutter again.

"Ooh sexy beast!" Reggie called after him. Flora hoped the detective hadn't heard the silly bird, as she blushed furiously and shushed her feathered companion with the promise of a few grapes.

THIRTY-FOUR

The week passed slowly from that point. Flora didn't see Bramble around the village, and assumed he was busy doing more formal interviews and working on other cases. The tearoom was quiet, so she spent a large portion of her time going through the black and white school photographs ready for the display on Saturday at her official opening event. Luckily they were all already backed in cardboard, as if they had been on display in the school at some point, so Flora simply had to choose which ones to use and where to display them around the walls. She couldn't face going up to the manor house and doing any more sorting.

Not many people had RSVP'd for the event, but Flora hoped there would be a good turnout on the day, nonetheless. She had been studiously avoiding Phil's texts offering help, as she hadn't quite worked out what to make of him yet, preferring to go through the pictures herself. Flora did feel a bit guilty though, as after all it had been Phil's idea and he had provided the photos. Not even the sweat-inducing first Baker's Rise Jazzercise class could pull Flora out of the funk she seemed to have fallen into. In fact, she felt that the hour's exercise nearly killed her and was seriously doubting whether she could go the next week. Tanya had been sweet and encouraging, though, and there were only four other women there for Flora to embarrass herself in front of. Tanya assured her that it would get easier with each week, but Flora wasn't so sure!

Her body protested any movement for the remainder of the week, so that when Saturday morning arrived, Flora was grumpier than ever. Even Reggie had started giving her a wide berth, sensing her mood.

Dressed in an expensive designer day dress of pale blue silk, with matching heels that Flora had had specially made at the time as the outfit was originally for a wedding, she was planning to go down to the tearoom early to check everything was in place. Lily

Houghton was bringing some jams and jars of honey from the farm shop before the event, to see if she could make a few sales too, as well as some home-baked goods which would be served on pretty, vintage china platters. George Jones was bringing a larger bakery order than usual, too, so Flora hoped she had the food side of things covered.

The day had dawned sunny and warm, and Flora toyed with the idea of wearing the hat which had accessorised the outfit for the original wedding. Deciding it was a step too far, and a bit too much for a village event of this size, she left the coach house without it, stepping out into the morning sunshine with Reggie flying ahead of her. It was the first time in the whole week – well, since she had last seen Bramble on Monday – that Flora had a spring in her step and a sense of hope that her tearoom venture would work out. Her novel had stalled at the planning stages so far, so she certainly couldn't rely on that for income any time soon.

It was after Lily had delivered a Tupperware box full of her delicious scones, along with a large carrot cake and some blueberry muffins, promising to return promptly for the event at eleven o'clock, that the bell above the door tinkled again. On seeing the new arrival, Reggie rose from his perch in a flurry of feathers, flapping around and squawking "the fool has arrived!" on repeat.

So, it wasn't until Flora managed to calm him that she saw her visitor was, in fact, Phil. Not understanding why her stomach sank slightly at his presence, or why she couldn't quite put a finger on what had gone wrong with their earlier easy friendship, Flora plastered a smile on her face in welcome.

Without so much as a hello, Phil cast a look around the room, all beautifully decorated for the event, "I see you got the photos up without me," he said, rather bluntly.

"I did, and don't they look great?" Flora tried to keep her voice light and airy, but inside she wondered why he had come earlier than the time on her invitations.

"They do. Look, Flora," Phil sighed, "I've been stressed out of my mind these last couple of weeks of term. But we broke up for the summer last Friday, so I was hoping we could get to know each other better over the school holidays?"

Flora studied his face for any sign of ulterior motive. *Since when did I become so suspicious?* she wondered. Perhaps it was this whole things with Harold's death, or spending time in Bramble's company. He always read between the lines. Was that what her mind was trying to do now? Read the subtext of Phil's sudden appearance?

"Phil, I'm rather busy," they both knew it was a lie, as the place was as pretty as a picture, and all the setting up had clearly been done – from the crisp white doilies on the tables, to the cake stands prepped for the onslaught of hungry villagers.

"Flora, please, I had hoped…"

"Listen, Phil, thanks for getting the school photos, but I wonder did you not have another reason for spending time with me? Perhaps you thought that if you got close to me, you could keep an eye on what I was finding up at The Rise? After all, you've known for weeks that I'm sorting through Harold's papers up there. Then there's the fact you saw him on the day he died, and that you were the recipient of some rather unpleasant mail from the man…"

Phil sucked in a large gulp of air, his hands balling into fists at his sides, and Flora knew she had gone too far.

"How did you find out about that?" Phil stuttered.

"I, well, I found some clippings that he'd used to create the messages, and then…. Well, let's just say I've come by quite a lot of information this past week." Flora took a couple of steps back, as Phil's eyes bored into hers. He looked like he was about to explode at any moment.

"Well, since you seem to know everything, Mrs. Miller, there's no point in my explaining myself! Except, that I want you to know what a terrible mistake you've made accusing me. Harold was a bast... a cheat and a liar. He tipped my late father over the edge into depression with his constant rent demands and refusal to fix the roof on my dad's cottage. Then, he tried to blackmail me after my dad's death by insinuating the man wasn't even my real father. I was angry, very angry, but..." he stopped himself then, his face red and his eyes glazed.

Flora stepped away from him, moving to place Reggie's perch between herself and this version of Phil which she didn't even recognise.

"Don't you feel safe with me, Flora?" he asked, almost sadly, but still with the clipped angry tone he had been using. An arm outstretched towards her, Phil had only taken one step in their direction when Reggie flew at him like a creature possessed, flapping his wings wildly, and aiming his beak at Phil's eyes. Phil used both his arms to cover his head, and ran from the tearoom, leaving the air blue with his bad language.

Flora sat heavily at the nearest table. Her legs felt like

jelly and her heart was beating wildly in her chest. She realised with sudden clarity that she'd just made a very silly mistake. If Phil was innocent of Harold's murder, then she'd surely just burnt all bridges with him. If he was guilty, then she had just tipped him off to both her knowledge and her suspicions, and in making him angry had surely set herself up as a target.

Reggie sat on the windowsill, as if on sentry duty, keeping guard. Flora wasn't aware of how long she sat, except that voices could be heard coming up the driveway when she finally dragged herself from her inner monologue. Her dress was crumpled where she had been wringing her hands on her lap and she had no idea how she was going to put a brave face on it and welcome her guests.

THIRTY-FIVE

Tanya took one look at Flora, and rushed straight to make her a cup of sweet tea. She had Shona with her, Ray Dodd's daughter, whom Flora had met at Jazzercise on Wednesday, and with them Shona's young son, Aaron. Pat wasn't with Tanya, and Flora didn't want to ask the lovely woman whether her husband still had the role of village policeman. In fact, Flora had rather come to the conclusion that she shouldn't go poking her nose into other people's business at all! Thankfully, Tanya had come early as she had promised to help Flora make and serve the drinks, so there weren't any other guests to worry about at the moment. By the time Flora had drunk the sweet tea and chatted with the women, while Aaron fussed over Reggie, who lapped up the attention, she felt much better.

"There," Tanya said, looking relieved, "the colour is back in your cheeks now! You mustn't worry about this 'grand opening' as you call it. All will be fine."

"Thank you, Tanya, I think my nerves just got the better of me."

As the tearoom began to fill up, Flora had no more time to ponder recent events. Billy Northcote arrived with Betty and Harry, George Jones arrived with his wife Pepper, Amy from the hairdresser's with her boyfriend, Gareth, and so on until the tiny tearoom was buzzing with activity. Reggie preened himself and fluffed up his feathers, behaving nicely as he relished the attention of so many guests at once, and Flora and Tanya floated around taking drinks orders and delivering food.

It was into this hubbub that Dr. and Mrs. Edwards arrived. Indeed, Flora did not see the couple until they were already looking at the school photos that were dotted around. The tables were all full, with more people standing, so Flora wasn't sure whether to offer them anything. She supposed she shouldn't be surprised, really, since they styled themselves as the king and queen of the village, that they should insist on attending every village event, whether they got on with the host or not. Clearly, they were here to have their faces seen, as they nodded politely in return to any greeting and made no move to congratulate Flora on what she had done with the place.

Flora was shocked, therefore, when Edwina tapped her firmly on the elbow as she passed with a tray of dirty crockery.

"Mrs. Miller," Edwina said haughtily, "how do I order a copy of this group photograph?"

Flora peered more closely at the picture in question as she replied, "You can order from the stall at the fete next month, this is just a small sample of the pictures available. Phil Drayford is organising the main thing, actually. Oh!" Flora looked from the photo to Edwina and then back again, "I did not know you had a sister?"

"A sister? No, I do not," Edwina said, before moving off to join her husband, leaving Flora none the wiser. As she peered at the picture, Flora couldn't get over how similar the young Edwina was to the girl sitting next to her. It was a whole school picture, so they perhaps weren't the same age, but that was clearly Edwina, her upturned nose and high cheekbones had not changed with the passing of time. But the girl next to her? Surely they must be related! Flora made a mental note to have a closer look at this photo after her guests had left.

Neither the vicar, nor his wife deigned to make an appearance, and Flora was glad of it. She basked in the compliments both on the tearoom's décor and on the quality of coffees and baked goods. Flora happily thanked Tanya and Lily as she made a small speech, welcoming everyone to the tearoom, and saying that she hoped all assembled would become firm regulars at the place, and also firm friends. The doctor and his wife had left by this point, having not lingered for more than a few minutes after making sure that their presence was noted. Flora was relieved, as she found Edwina Edwards to be a rude, suffocating woman. Here, in her own little space, Flora decided there and then that she would no longer feel like an outsider. She had made friends, she thought, as she looked at the smiling faces of Betty and Harry, of Billy Northcote, Tanya, Shona and Lily. Even Stan had left the farm for the occasion, and managed to have a wash and clean up too, by the looks of it! Yes, Flora decided, she was welcome here, and she would make a good go of it.

The shadow of her earlier confrontation with Phil loomed over her, as Flora began the large task of clearing up, but she was determined not to let it ruin an otherwise enjoyable and successful day. She had assured Tanya and Lily that she needed no help with the washing up and wiping down, so it was just Flora and Reggie left in the small tearoom as the sun began to lower in the sky. It was then that Flora remembered the strange interaction with Edwina, and she went to the photo and unstuck it from the wall carefully. Peeling back the faded cardboard backing, Flora was excited to see a list of names, and a date, all handwritten in a cursive script with black ink. Scrolling through, Flora found Edwina – Green as she had then been known – and next to hers, a name which Flora also recognised.

THIRTY-SIX

Flora decided to skip church the next morning, as she was eager to head up to the manor house and look through the files in the secret room more thoroughly. Indeed, she had one person in particular whom she wished to learn more about, before calling Detective Bramble with news of what she had found. She certainly had no plans to go in alone and with all guns blazing as she had yesterday! Some of Bramble's team were coming to the big house the next day to begin the job of sorting through the secret room, so Flora was aware she didn't have much time to investigate alone.

The sun of the previous day had disappeared behind a pall of clouds as Flora and Reggie walked up the driveway to The Rise. The tearoom was closed on

Sundays, as the village traditionally held the day as a time of rest. As the majority of her new friends would be attending the service, Flora was content that she would have a few undisturbed hours to spend on her explorations.

Letting them in at the side door as usual, Flora was happy when Reggie didn't fly immediately to the sitting room at the front of the house. The police tape had been removed from that doorway, but she imagined the room still smelt of the chemicals and suchlike that the forensics team had used, and she didn't want her feathered friend unsettled by them. Instead, they both went into the large back study together, and Flora took the overflowing bucket to empty in the kitchen sink. There hadn't been enough rain lately to cause a leak this big, so Flora surmised that a water tank in the roof space above the room must be leaking and decided regretfully that she must make it a priority to get this fixed when her divorce money came through. Certainly, the ceiling bulge looked much worse than the last time she had been here, with Detective Bramble.

Placing the empty bucket back under the drips, Flora spent some time stacking the remainder of the papers on the floor into neat piles. It didn't actually remove any from the room, or really sort anything, but it gave the illusion of organisation and made her feel better. Reggie was perched on the mantle, and rubbed his head into Flora's hand affectionately when she came over to pull the large wooden candlestick so as to release the secret door.

It was in this moment, that Flora became aware of another presence in the room. A sickly sweet scent had filled the air, and Reggie's happy chirps had stopped abruptly. Out of the corner of her eye, spying the well-dressed woman with bright red lipstick, Flora assumed it was Edwina Edwards, though what the doctor's wife could possibly want up here, Flora had no idea. It wasn't until she turned to fully face the intruder, that Flora realised with a start that it wasn't Edwina at all.

"Silly old trout!" Reggie squawked, becoming suddenly on edge and restless, his wings flapping on the spot.

"Will they not miss you in the church?" Flora asked, willing her voice to remain calm and neutral.

"I feigned an attack of fainting just before the service began. They think I am resting in the vestry. The perfect alibi."

"Alibi for what?"

The woman cackled, not an attractive sound, more like a bird being slowly strangled, "Don't act obtuse, Mrs. Miller, you know fine well why I'm here. I can't have you investigating Harold's death any further, now can I?" The malice sparkled in the woman's eyes, and Flora wondered in that moment if she wasn't quite mad.

"I have no idea what you mean, Enid. It is Enid, isn't it, under all of that disguise? You look much different when you're not in your dowdy garb of vicar's wife, much more like your cousin, Edwina!"

Enid drew in a sharp breath, but said nothing, so Flora ploughed on, eager to buy some time, but for what she wasn't sure.

"I've seen a picture of you both as children – you could be twins! Now, with your blonde wig and heavily made-up face, anyone casting just a passing glance would assume you were one and the same person. Tell me, why did you kill Harold? Was it because of his blackmailing your husband over the church roof fraud?"

"The church roof? Pah! That little money-making scheme is Francis' own. No, Harold had to go because he caused me the ultimate embarrassment at last year's fete."

"You can't surely be talking about the Scone Competition?"

"Indeed I am," she was shouting now, "I was robbed! There is no way Betty Lafferty should have taken first place with that monstrosity. It wasn't even a traditional recipe!"

"But how did you know about the peanut allergy?"

"Oh, I've known about that for years. At another fete a way back I made a peanut brittle, and the stupid man refused to taste it when judging the Tasty Treats competition, said it contained peanut and that even a tiny taste would make him sick. Of course it contained peanut, it's in the name! Wouldn't even touch it!"

Enid was advancing towards Flora now. She grabbed the iron poker from the side of the fireplace and lunged.

In that moment, Reggie flew at the woman, wings flapping wildly. He swooped upwards until he hit the sagging ceiling, in an attempt to then divebomb the intruder. He didn't need to bother, however, as his efforts brought down the whole of the damp ceiling onto Enid, and partially on Flora, who had tried to jump away at the last minute. With a shriek, Enid collapsed under the falling masonry, as dust filled the room, and Flora's vision went black.

THIRTY-SEVEN

Flora sat up in her hospital bed, her head throbbing. She rubbed her eyes, still half-closed from sleep, and noticed a familiar form in the chair in the corner of the room.

"Detective Bramble," Flora said, happy to see the man despite the fact she knew she must look a sight.

"Flora, how are you feeling? You took quite a hit to the head from that ceiling falling yesterday."

"Reggie! Where is he?" Flora asked, immediately concerned as the events of the previous day came flooding back

"He's at the coach house with Tanya. I found the door

keys in your handbag. She said to tell you that everything is fine, she'll open the tearoom today, and she's had a great idea of what you can do with all your clothes. She said you'd know what she meant, and just to say that it involves next month's fete!"

"Oh, she's a star, thank you Detective" Flora said, as Bramble moved his chair closer to the bed and tentatively took her hand in his.

"Please, call me Adam," his thumb ran lightly over Flora's palm, "I'm off duty, and you gave me such a fright yesterday when I thought… well, I thought something bad had happened to you. It was lucky that Billy Northcote was out back in the rose garden and heard the loud crash of the ceiling coming down or…" his voice cracked.

"What about Enid, did she…?"

"Survive? Yes. She has several cracked ribs, a concussion and a broken hip and arm, but she will live. She was babbling away when they put her in the ambulance. All about Harold's murder and some scone competition. Blackett is taking her statement now. She's under room arrest here at the hospital. But don't worry you're safe now."

"I feel safe. You make me feel safe," Flora whispered,

and she looked into his warm eyes and breathed a sigh of thanks that her investigating days were now over.

Join Flora and Reggie in "Pie Comes Before a Fall", the next instalment in the Baker's Rise Mysteries, to see whether her investigating days really have come to an end!

ABOUT THE AUTHOR

Rachel Hutchins lives in northeast England with her husband, three children and their dog Boudicca. She loves writing both mysteries and romances, and enjoys reading these genres too! Her favourite place is walking along the local coastline, with a coffee and some cake!

You can connect with Rachel and sign up to her monthly newsletter via her website at: www.authorrachelhutchins.com

Alternatively, she has social media pages on:

Facebook: www.facebook.com/rahutchinsauthor

Instagram: www.instagram.com/ra_hutchins_author

Twitter: www.twitter.com/hutchinsauthor

OTHER BOOKS BY R. A. HUTCHINS

"Counting down to Christmas"

Rachel has published a collection of twelve contemporary romance stories, all set around Christmas, and with the common theme of a holiday happily-ever-after. Filled with humour and emotion, they are sure to bring a sparkle to your day!

"To Catch A Feather" (Found in Fife Book One)

When tragedy strikes an already vulnerable Kate Winters, she retreats into herself, broken and beaten. Existing rather than living, she makes a journey North to try to find herself, or maybe just looking for some sort of closure.

Cameron McAllister has known his own share of grief and love lost. His son, Josh, is now his only priority. In his forties and running a small coffee shop in a tiny Scottish fishing village, Cal knows he is unlikely to find love again.

When the two meet and sparks fly, can they overcome their past losses and move on towards a shared future, or are the memories which haunt them still too real?

These books, as well as others by Rachel, can be found on Amazon worldwide in e-book and paperback formats, as well as free to read on Kindle Unlimited.

R. A. Hutchins

Printed in Great Britain
by Amazon

34451041R00149